That was when he reached out and grabbed her by the arms.

He did it gently. But the sudden move surprised her nonetheless.

Marnie stopped laughing. She stared up into his leaf-green eyes. She heard herself whisper, "Jericho…"

And then she understood. Out of nowhere, it all fell into place for her.

He…liked her. In *that* way. He wanted her.

The very idea seemed completely impossible—and yet so deeply satisfying, both at the same time.

Because, well, she wanted him, too. She hadn't realized it until that moment, when he grabbed her and looked down into her eyes and everything suddenly shifted, when she saw that all of it, this edgy thing between them, made the most amazing kind of sense.

Dear Reader,

After a seriously rocky start, Jericho Bravo has turned his life around. He's healed the rift with his family and found honest work that suits him perfectly.

Marnie Jones was once a wild child. Not anymore. She flees to Texas in her battered old car with five hundred dollars to her name. Her goal: to heal her broken heart and to find the true self she somehow lost along the way.

Neither Marnie nor Jericho is looking for love. Especially not with each other. He's a loner, and the one thing she doesn't need is a new man in her life.

But love has a funny way of popping up in the most unlikely places. And sometimes the last person a woman could ever see herself falling for turns out to be just the man for her.

Happy reading, everyone.

Yours always,

Christine Rimmer

A BRIDE FOR JERICHO BRAVO

CHRISTINE RIMMER

Silhouette

SPECIAL EDITION

Published by Silhouette Books

America's Publisher of Contemporary Romance

SILHOUETTE BOOKS

ISBN-13: 978-0-373-65511-3

Recycling programs
for this product may
not exist in your area.

A BRIDE FOR JERICHO BRAVO

This edition published by arrangement with Harlequin Books S.A.

For questions and comments about the quality of this book please contact us at Customer_eCare@Harlequin.ca.

® and TM are trademarks of Harlequin Books S.A., used under license. Trademarks indicated with ® are registered in the United States Patent and Trademark Office, the Canadian Trade Marks Office and in other countries.

Visit Silhouette Books at www.eHarlequin.com

Printed in U.S.A.

Books by Christine Rimmer

CHRISTINE RIMMER

came to her profession the long way around. Before settling down to write about the magic of romance, she'd been everything from an actress to a salesclerk to a waitress. Now that she's finally found work that suits her perfectly, she insists she never had a problem keeping a job—she was merely gaining "life experience" for her future as a novelist. Christine is grateful not only for the joy she finds in writing, but for what waits when the day's work is through: a man she loves, who loves her right back, and the privilege of watching their children grow and change day to day. She lives with her family in Oklahoma. Visit Christine at www.christinerimmer.com.

For MSR, always.

Chapter One

It was a very bad day in a very bad week in what would no doubt turn into a really rotten month. Otherwise, Marnie Jones would never have stolen that chopper. Plus, there was Jericho Bravo. First, he scared her to death. And then he made her mad.

Really mad. And he did it at the end of her very bad day. His making her mad was the final straw, or so she told herself when she hot-wired that beautiful motorcycle.

If she hadn't been feeling so crazy, so desperate and miserable, she might have been able to be more objective about the whole thing. She might have reminded herself that it wasn't his fault that he had scared her silly. And when he made her mad, well, he was only telling the truth as he saw it.

But she *was* feeling crazy and desperate and miserable. That day, she was in no mood to be objective about anything.

The very bad day in question? It was April 1. So appropriate. On the day for fools, Marnie knew herself to be the biggest fool of all.

The day before, Wednesday, March 31, her life had imploded when Mark Drury broke up with her. Mark was not only her live-in lover of five years, but he was also her best friend in the world since childhood, her blood brother since the age of nine.

The house they shared in Santa Barbara belonged to him. So when he dumped her, she had nowhere to go and no best friend to talk to. She threw all her things in the back of her old black Camry and got out of there.

She started to go home—home being the tiny town of North Magdalene northeast of Sacramento, in the Sierras. But after about ten minutes behind the wheel, she realized that she simply couldn't do it, couldn't go back there. Couldn't face the worry in her dad's eyes, the tender sympathy her stepmother would offer, the endless advice of her crazy Grandpa Oggie. Couldn't stand to be the one the whole town was talking about.

Yeah, she knew they would only be talking about her because they cared for her. But still. She couldn't take the humiliation.

So instead of heading north, she went east. She had no idea why, no clue where she was going. Just somewhere that wasn't Santa Barbara or North Magdalene.

Seven hours later, as she rolled into Phoenix, her destination became clear. She was going to San Antonio, going to her big sister, Tessa.

She kept driving. After thirteen hours on the road, she reached El Paso. It was getting dark. She got a burger and fries from a drive-through, found a cheap motel and checked in for the night.

She tried to sleep. Not happening. And her cell kept ringing. It was Mark. She didn't answer, just let his calls go to voicemail and then deleted them without listening to them. She didn't need to hear him say he only wanted to be sure that she was all right. She wasn't all right. She didn't think she would ever be all right again. And he, of all people, ought to know that.

At dawn, she dragged herself out of the motel bed and started driving.

She made it to San Antonio at ten past noon. Fifteen minutes later, she was pulling up in front of her sister's new place, a gorgeous Spanish-style house in a very pricey neighborhood called Olmos Park.

Marnie's big sister, notorious in North Magdalene for her bad luck with men, had finally found the guy for her. His name was Ash Bravo. Ash was killer-hot and he had lots of money. But what really mattered was that he was long-gone, over-the-moon in love with Tessa—as she was, with him. They'd been married for two years now and had recently moved from his house, in another high-priced area of San Antonio, to this one, which they'd chosen as a couple.

Marnie sat in the car for a while, thinking of how she probably should have called her sister first, given Tessa a little warning, at least. Somehow, she just hadn't been able to bring herself to dial her sister's number. There was too much to explain. Marnie hardly knew where to start.

Eventually, she shoved open her door, shouldered

her purse and got out of the car. Her legs felt kind of rubbery and her head swam. She'd had nothing to eat since that greasy burger the night before. She shut the door and braced both hands on the dusty black roof of the Camry. Head drooping, she took a few slow, deep breaths as she waited for the light-headedness to pass.

When she looked up again, a skinny, fortyish, deeply tanned woman in cross-trainers, bike shorts and an exercise bra jogged past across the street. The woman frowned in Marnie's direction. Marnie couldn't really blame her. She knew she looked like hell and her car was old and dusty, the backseat packed with just about everything she owned. The skinny woman probably thought she was some homeless person.

Which, come to think of it, she was.

The realization brought a laugh to Marnie's lips, a brittle, angry sound. The woman in the cross-trainers ran faster, quickly disappearing around the corner.

Marnie pulled herself up straight, turned and started up the long, winding front walk, which curved beneath the dappled shade of a pair of handsome pecan trees, their branches arching prettily to mesh like joined hands overhead. Attractive flower beds flanked the wide, red-tiled front step and the outer door was of iron lace. Marnie rang the bell.

A few moments later, the inner door swung inward. Tessa stood there, in jeans and a pretty gauze shirt. Her hazel eyes darkened. She sucked in a small, shocked gasp.

"Marnie…?"

"Hey."

Tessa pushed open the outer door. "Marnie. What in the…?"

"I couldn't make myself go home. And I didn't know where else to go."

Tessa did just the right thing then. She held out her arms.

By three that afternoon, Marnie still felt like crap. But marginally better crap.

Tessa had let her cry, listened to her long sad story, fed her lunch and given her a space to park her Camry in the five-car detached garage behind the house. She'd also helped Marnie carry her stuff along the walk that circled the pool to the guesthouse out in back. It was a cute little two-bedroom stone cottage, a much-smaller version of the main house, complete with a bright, galley-style kitchen and a nice view of the pool.

"Take a long, hot shower," Tessa instructed after helping her put her things away. "And maybe a nap."

"I could sleep straight through till tomorrow."

"Dinner first. You need to eat."

"You sound like Gina, you know that?" Regina Black Jones was their stepmother. She had married their father when Tessa was twelve and Marnie, nine.

Tessa laughed. "Gina was the best thing that ever happened to us."

"I know. Regular meals. Rules. And a boatload of unconditional love."

"We needed her then." *Just like I need you now.* "Tessa?"

"Um?"

"Thank you."

"Thanks are never necessary. I'm here, always. For you." Tessa stroked her hair. "You'll be okay."

Marnie answered with more confidence than she felt. "I know."

"A long, hot shower. And then rest. Dinner around seven or so. Just family, nothing fancy. You and me and Ash and Jericho."

"Jericho. One of the brothers?" It was a big family. Ash had six brothers. And two sisters. And also a half sister named Elena.

Tessa was nodding. "Jericho is sixth-born. After Caleb, before Travis."

"Ah." Marnie had met Ash's family at the wedding. But that was two years ago. There were a lot of Bravos and they all kind of blurred together in her mind.

Tessa cupped her face, kissed her on the cheek and left her alone.

Peeling off her road-wrinkled clothes as she went, Marnie headed for the bathroom. After her shower, she stretched out on the sofa, where she could look out the French doors at the gleaming pool and the main house beyond. She closed her eyes and tried to sleep, but sheer exhaustion had every nerve humming. And in spite of the big lunch Tessa had insisted she eat, she felt hollow inside.

Her cell rang. She grabbed her purse off the coffee table, fished out her phone and saw it was Mark. Again. He wasn't going to stop calling until he knew she was safe.

With a sigh, she pushed the talk button and put it to her ear. "Do you mind? Leave me alone."

"I just want to know that you're all—"

"All right?" She made a hard, snorting sound. "Well, I'm not. But I'm safe. I'm at Tessa's."

"Tessa's." He sounded stunned. As if she'd caught a flight to the moon or something. "You went all the way to Texas."

"Stop calling me. I mean it. I'm alive. I'm okay. And I'm none of your damn business. Ever again."

"Marnie—"

"Leave me alone."

"Marnie, I—"

"Say it. I mean it. Just say you will leave me alone."

"I—"

"Say it, Mark!" She shouted the demand into the phone.

A silence. And then, at last, "All right. I'll stop calling."

"Good. Goodbye." She disconnected before he could say any more. Then she powered the phone off and tossed it on the coffee table next to her purse.

She flopped back to the couch cushions and shut her eyes. She didn't expect to sleep. But she did. Like a rock dropping into a bottomless well, darkness sucked her down.

A loud rumbling sound woke her.

For a moment, she thought maybe there was an earthquake.

But then, groggily, she remembered where she was: not California. Tessa's. In San Antonio.

It all came flooding back, in total awfulness. Mark had dumped her. She'd fled to Texas…

The rumbling sound died away. Probably some motorcycle out on the street.

She grabbed her phone, powered it on and checked

the time. Six-thirty. A half hour till dinner. So she got up, brushed her hair, put on some lip gloss, grabbed her purse and headed back over to the main house.

The charming rock path went both ways around the pool. For a little variety, she crossed around away from the garage that time, pausing to watch fat koi gliding beneath the surface in a pond near the far fence and to take comfort from the soothing sound of the small waterfall that gurgled over rough black rocks.

She went in through French doors to the kitchen, where the walls were a warm gold, the counters of brightly painted Spanish tile and the appliances chef-quality. Tessa's old, nearly deaf bulldog, Mona Lou, was asleep in a dog bed in the corner. The dog got up, stretched and waddled over for a pat on the head. When she whined, Marnie opened the door again and let her out into the backyard.

Something was cooking. It smelled really good. Her stomach grumbled, so she grabbed a banana from the big fruit bowl on the counter.

Munching the banana, looking for Tessa and Ash, she left the kitchen and wandered through the empty family room, where Tessa's white cat Gigi was sleeping on the couch. Gigi lifted her head and squinted at Marnie as she went by.

Everything was so quiet. Had they left suddenly, for some reason? She paused at the curving iron-railed staircase in the foyer and glanced up toward the top floor, but didn't mount the stairs. Maybe Ash and Tessa were up there, sharing a private moment before dinner.

The doors to the study stood open. She finished off the last of her banana, set her purse on the entry table and poked her head in there. It was a masculine refuge, with a beautiful old desk and credenza of the same dark, rich wood and tall, carved mahogany bookcases rising to the cove ceiling. Still wondering where everyone had gone, she turned for the living room across the foyer, her footfalls echoing softly on the hardwood floor.

She didn't see the man until she'd reached the open archway that led into the large, bright room. He stood over by the fireplace with his back to her, his long, dark brown hair tied in a ponytail with a strip of leather, wearing a gray T-shirt, faded, torn jeans and heavy boots.

Even from behind, he looked menacing. He was at least six-three, with a neck like a linebacker and massive tattooed arms straining the sleeves of his T-shirt. She could even see the pointed black edges of a tattoo rising out of his collar at the nape of his neck.

Maybe it was the silence of the beautiful house, the unexpected absence of Tessa and Ash. Maybe it was the recent collapse of her life as she had come to know it. Maybe it was his size, the sense of power and strength and danger that seemed to radiate off him. Maybe it was simply her surprise at seeing him there, looking so out of place in her sister's pretty, upscale living room.

Whatever the reason, a sudden terror filled her. An icy shiver cut a frozen path of mindless fear down her spine, along her thighs, outward over the surface of her arms.

He turned toward her. She saw his face, which was surprisingly handsome for someone so large and scary. He opened his mouth to speak.

She still had the banana peel clutched in her hand. She threw it at him and started screaming.

* * *

Feet on the upper floor, running.

She whirled to see her sister and Ash coming at her down the iron-railed staircase.

"Marnie," Tessa cried. "Marnie, what is it? What's wrong?"

In seconds they were both at her side. By then, she had stopped screaming. Tessa grabbed her and pulled her close.

She huddled against her sister, already beginning to realize that the man by the fireplace wasn't an intruder after all. If he had been, he would have done something other than stand there and glare at her.

Then Ash spoke to him. "Jericho, what's going on?"

Jericho.

The brother. The brother who was coming to dinner. She should have known that, shouldn't she?

"What's going on?" The big man echoed Ash's question in a voice every bit as deep and rough as she would have expected. "How the hell would I know what's going on? She saw me and she started screaming."

Marnie let out a small whimper of abject embarrassment. "Oh, God…"

He held up the banana peel. "She threw this at me. Luckily, I ducked." He kind of squinted at her. She saw humor in his green eyes—and anger, too. He was trying not to let the anger show. But she recognized it. He didn't like that she'd mistaken him for some kind of thug.

She pulled away from Tessa and made herself stand up straight. "I, um, I'm really sorry. The house was so quiet. And…you surprised me, that's all."

"Yeah?" He came closer. The look in his eyes said she better not shrink away.

She didn't, even though instinct had the skin at the back of her neck pulling tight. He was proud, she knew that, could read it in his eyes, in the way he carried himself. The kind of guy you shouldn't cross. Or embarrass. She forced a wobbly smile and confessed, "It wasn't you. It was me. I've had a…rough couple of days…"

He reached out. She was very careful not to flinch when he took her hand in his big, rough paw. He slapped the banana peel into it.

"Uh. Thanks," she said, because she couldn't think of anything else to say.

And then Tessa started talking, urging them fully into the living room. She took Marnie's hand, but only to whisk the banana peel away. Ash gave her a hug and said he was happy to see her, then he went to the wet bar on the inside wall of the big room to pour margaritas from the icy pitcher waiting there. He gave them each a glass of the frozen concoction. Except for Tessa. She had sparkling water.

They all took seats. Marnie got a wing chair to herself. She leaned back in it and sipped her drink and tried to think of something interesting to say.

Nothing came to her, so she was quiet. The other three talked, about how good the house looked. About the family company, BravoCorp, of which Ash was CEO. About Jericho's business, San Antonio Choppers, which he ran in partnership with somebody named Gus. He built custom motorcycles, she learned.

When she thought he wasn't looking, she studied

him and tried to remember meeting him at Tessa and Ash's wedding. She couldn't recall ever seeing him before. Maybe he hadn't been there. Because really, he wasn't the kind of guy a person forgets.

Once, as she sneaked a glance at him, he caught her at it. He looked straight at her then, green eyes dark and deep as a mountain lake where no one ever goes. Cold. Wild. Untouched.

Marnie blinked first. She turned away and found her sister looking at her. Tessa smiled. A tender smile—and a worried one. Then Ash said something. And Jericho said something. The conversation continued without her.

After the margaritas, Tessa led them to the dining room, where the table was set for four. She brought in the food from the kitchen and Ash opened wine. Only the men drank it. Tessa was sticking with sparkling water. And the last thing Marnie needed was to get blasted on top of everything else.

Most of the conversation centered on some big charity event that was set for the first of May. Jericho was offering one of his custom bikes to be auctioned off for the cause. Ash seemed very pleased over this— even excited. Jericho only shrugged a giant shoulder and said he was glad to help.

Marnie hardly said a word. Encased in her own private cloud of misery, she tuned out the others and picked at the excellent dinner.

Dessert came. Some sort of slippery, cinnamon-flavored flan thing, really good, like the rest of the meal had been. She ate a few bites of it, to be polite.

Finally, after what seemed like a long and excessively grim lifetime, the meal was over. The men went to Ash's study and Marnie helped Tessa clean up—or tried to.

"Leave it for now," Tessa said, when they had carried the plates to the kitchen. "The housekeeper will take care of it all in the morning, anyway. You go ahead to bed, get some rest."

Marnie slowly shook her head. "I feel really bad about Ash's brother…."

Tessa reached out and touched the side of her face with a tender hand. "Don't. You're tired and on edge. You need a good night's sleep."

"I think he hates me now."

"Of course he doesn't."

"And I embarrassed Ash. And you."

"Marnie."

"What?"

"Go to bed. It'll all look better in the morning."

She blew out a hard sigh. "Yeah. I'm sure you're right." She got a last hug from her sister and left as she had entered, through the French doors, going around by the pond again, not as comforted by the chuckling fountain as she had been earlier.

In the larger of the guesthouse bedrooms, she put on her sleep shirt and trudged into the bathroom to brush her teeth. She really looked awful, bags under her bloodshot eyes, her skin kind of splotchy. Way too pale. Even her hair seemed depressed. It hung limp as a dirty brown curtain to her shoulders.

She made herself not look at the mirror again as she squirted toothpaste on her toothbrush and cleaned her teeth. Then it was back to the bedroom and the nice, fresh white sheets on the comfy bed. She climbed in and pulled the covers over her and shut her eyes.

And remembered that she'd left her purse in the house.

Why had she taken it over there, anyway? She had no idea. She hadn't needed it then—and she didn't really need it now.

But then, it did have her phone in it. What if someone called her? Other than Mark. What if *she* needed to make a call?

True, there was a landline on the nightstand—and no, she couldn't think of a single person she wanted to call. And yet…

Fine. She would get the damn purse.

She shoved back the covers, pulled her jeans back on under the sleep shirt and stuck her feet in a pair of flip-flops. That time she went around in front of the garage to get to the back door, so she saw Jericho's chopper parked in the turnaround area between the house and the garage. It was beautiful, big and black with metal-flake cobalt-blue trim and shiny chrome. Even in the shadows of twilight the gorgeous thing gleamed, its stretched front forks looking so danger-ous—and fast.

The sight of it made her throat clutch, brought a sharp pang of longing for home, where her dad ran the local garage, had since she was a kid. Sometimes bikers would bring their choppers in when something went wrong during a mountain ride.

Once, before she and Mark started dating, when he was only her blood brother and very best friend, one of those bikers had taken her for a ride. It was thrilling and scary, rounding sharp mountain turns, the wind tearing at her, blowing her hair out from under her borrowed helmet, as the bike picked up speed.

She remembered the biker's laughter, blown back to her on the wind, the smell of road dust and pine forest all around, the engine roaring in her ears, vibrating through her body, making her feel a little afraid, stunningly alive. And utterly free.

What happened to you? Mark's voice. Filling her head, saying all the cruel things he'd said yesterday morning. *Marnie, I hardly know you anymore. You used to take chances. You used to be willing to rise to any challenge, the bravest girl I ever knew. Where did that girl go? I think you need to find out. Marnie, I think that you and me, we're not meant to be. Not in this way. I think you need to ask yourself. Where is your spark?*

Shut up, Mark.

She shook herself and turned away from the beautiful bike, toward the main house again.

Tessa wasn't in the kitchen. The dishes they'd brought in from the dining room waited on the counter, just as they'd left them. Marnie went through the family room where the white cat still slept and down the hall to the foyer to get her purse from the entry table.

The doors to the study were open. She could hear voices in there, male voices: Ash and his brother. She would have to cross the open doorway to get her purse. The thought of doing that, of having the two men see her and wonder what she was doing wandering around the main house without Tessa, made her nervous— which only proved Mark was right about her. She was scared of her own damn shadow.

Where had her brave self gone?

As she hovered there at the foot of the stairs, admitting how pitiful and silly she was being, she heard Jericho's rough voice, painfully clear, from inside the study.

"No, man. I mean really. You probably ought to get her to a shrink or something."

Ash said, "She'll be fine. She's had a rough couple of days, that's all."

"She didn't say a word through dinner. Just sat there, staring. Didn't you notice?"

"Rico. Come on."

"She got a drug problem, maybe?"

"Her boyfriend dumped her and she drove all the way here from Santa Barbara. She's beat and her life's in chaos. And you scared her."

"I didn't do crap. I was just standing there. That woman is not okay, I'm telling you. She needs—"

Marnie didn't stick around to hear what she needed— let alone, to get her purse. Her cheeks burning and her heart pounding hard and fast with shame and fury, she whirled to go back the way she had come, pausing only to yank off her flip-flops so neither Ash nor his bigmouth butthead of a brother would hear her retreat.

Barefoot, clutching her flip-flops in her fist, she took off down the hall, racing through the family room and the kitchen and, at last, out the French doors to the backyard. Once outside in the gathering dark, she stopped and sucked in a few deep breaths of the cool night air.

The deep breaths didn't help much. Her heart still knocked against her ribs like it wanted to break right through the wall of her chest. Her cheeks still flamed with humiliation. She started running again, not quite so fast now, jogging back the way she had come.

The chopper was still waiting there, chrome shining, metal flake blue giving off a kind of sparkle even in the growing darkness. She slowed as she approached it and then veered toward it instead of running on by. A helmet waited on the seat.

In her head, Jericho's voice now warred with Mark's.

She got a drug problem, maybe?

What happened to you?

You probably ought to get her to a shrink or something.

You used to take chances.

That woman is not okay, I am telling you.

…willing to rise to any challenge. The bravest girl I ever knew.

…didn't say a word through dinner.

I think you have to ask yourself…

Just sat there, staring…

Where is your spark?

Marnie put on her flip-flops.

Her spark? Mark wanted to know what had happened to her spark?

Well, maybe she'd just show him. Maybe she would show them all, on Jericho's fancy bike. Maybe she would take that chopper for a nice, long ride.

Yeah, okay. She knew it was a bad idea. A very bad idea.

It was not only dangerous, it was also grand theft.

Where is your spark?

She'd learned a thing or two back in North Magdalene, in her dad's garage. Like how to start an engine without a key.

The job required something to pry with. So she hustled into the garage, flip-flops slapping concrete as she went, and got a screwdriver from the tool kit she kept in her trunk. Once she had that, she ran back outside. She stuck the screwdriver in a pocket, grabbed the helmet and put it on. It was too big, but she tightened the strap as much as she could.

Squeezing the right brake lever to avoid any surprise wheelies, she straddled the bike and eased it upright between her legs. From atop the beautiful machine, it was a long way down those front forks to the front wheel.

In fact, the bike seemed bigger, now she was straddling it. Really big. And really dangerous. Even if she could get it started, the thing weighed more than she did and it would be a stretch for her feet to reach the pegs. It was way too much bike for her to handle....

She shut her eyes tight and called up Mark's words in her mind.

Where is your spark?

When she opened her eyes again, she was ready. She was going to do it. She would not wimp out.

Using her heel, she guided the side stand up. She put the bike in neutral, released her grip on the brake and walked it around so it faced the driveway on the side of the house.

Then she turned the fuel valve to the on position and used her screwdriver to pry off the metal ignition cap, revealing the battery and ignition wires.

After that, it was so simple. She stuck the screwdriver in one back pocket and the ignition cap in the other and she twisted those wires together.

The big engine roared to life. She turned on the lights, pressed the clutch, shifted into gear and eased the clutch out as she gave it gas.

*He then faced forward so fast. She tried to see in the fading sunlight she stood with her head and shoulders.
The shout silenced her protest.*

Chapter Two

"**D**id you hear that?" Jericho frowned at his brother.

The sudden roar began to travel. It rumbled along the side of the house, back to front.

"Sounds like your bike," Ash said, looking puzzled.

Jericho glanced over his brother's shoulder, out the window that faced the front of the house, just in time to see Tessa's crazy sister rolling off down the street under the golden light of the streetlamps. She was riding his bike.

He said, "Your sister-in-law just stole my bike."

Ash looked at him like *he* was the one with a screw loose.

Jericho decided not to argue. "I need to borrow a car."

"Rico…"

"A car, Ash. Now."

Ash let out a weary sigh and fished a set of keys from his pocket. "The Mercedes. First door on the end, by the fence."

It took a few minutes to get to the Mercedes, get it started, get the garage door up and get rolling. That was a few minutes too long, as far as Jericho was concerned.

By the time he reached the street, Tessa's disturbed sister was long gone. He rolled down all the windows so he could hear the bike if he got anywhere near it and he turned the car in the direction she'd been headed when she passed in front of Ash's study.

At the corner, a T intersection, he took a wild guess and went right, figuring a rider unfamiliar with a big bike would take the easy turn, given a choice. After that, he went straight until the fork in the road, where he veered to the right again and tried not to think about the damage that could be done to an expensive piece of machinery with a crazy woman riding it.

And what about the crazy woman herself? What could happen to her was even scarier. At least she'd been wearing his helmet when she drove past the front window. If she ended up eating pavement, she might break every bone in her skinny little body—but just maybe she wouldn't kill herself.

He kept going, ears tuned for the bike's distinctive sound. As he turned the circle around a doughnut intersection where five streets came together, he heard the familiar rumble.

From there, he just followed the sound.

He caught up with her as she turned—right again—

onto the street that circled the park. She wasn't going very fast, which was really good news. Plus, the street was essentially deserted. Two pickups went past going the opposite direction, headlights cutting the thickening darkness. But no vehicles blocked the space between the Mercedes and the bike.

Once he found her, it was simple. He got a bit too close, showing her some wheel, and she guided the bike nearer to the curb, wobbling a little as she went, to let him pass.

But he didn't pass. He just got up parallel with her and drove along at a matching crawl. Any slower and she'd kill that big engine. In fact, how she'd managed not to kill it before then was a mystery to him.

She glanced over, her face all pinched and pissed off inside his too-big helmet. And she saw it was him. The surprise on her face might have been funny, if he hadn't been more than a little freaked that she would hit the gas and lose control.

But the fates were kind. The sight of him had her easing off the throttle rather than gunning it. The bike sputtered and died. She rolled toward the shoulder. When the bike stopped, she put her feet down. He pulled the Mercedes in behind her.

Leaving the car's engine running and the headlights on to see by, he was out the door and heading for her as she lowered the stand and climbed off. She undid the helmet strap. Her light brown hair caught static and crackled when she lifted the helmet free of her head.

He reached her. Moving slowly and carefully, she set the helmet on the seat. And then she turned and met his eyes. He had all kinds of things he was going to yell at her, all kinds of names he was going to call her.

But those big blue eyes looked so sad and so lost, he forgot about how he thought she was crazy. He even let go of the proud rage she had stirred in him when she took him for a burglar in his own brother's house.

It seemed only natural. Just to hold out his arms. She stared at him for a moment, a small space of time that somehow became endless. In the headlight's hard glare, her expression showed surprise. And then, in an instant, acceptance.

With a heavy sigh, she sagged against him. He gathered her in.

A couple more cars went by as they stood there, embracing in the wash of bright light. She hooked her arms around his waist and buried her face against his chest. A soft, wordless sound escaped her. He felt the warmth of her breath, easing its way through the cloth of his shirt, touching his flesh.

And then she pulled back. He had the strangest urge to keep holding on. But he tamped that urge down. He let her go and she stepped away.

She hung her head. "I didn't even have the guts to go fast."

"And that's a good thing." He spoke sternly. "It would have been a seriously bad idea to do that."

"Yeah. I guess." She pulled something from her back pocket and held it out. It was the bike's ignition cap.

He took it from her, suddenly remembering that her father was a mechanic. He'd met Patrick Jones at Ash's wedding. "Your dad runs a garage, right?"

"Uh-huh. He taught me a thing or two about engines. Enough to make me dangerous, I guess." She was still looking down, subdued now.

He just didn't get it. "I gotta ask. What's this about? Why would you steal my bike? What's the point?"

She shook her head. "It's a long story."

"Try me."

"My boyfriend dumped me."

"I heard. I'm sorry. But…why take it out on me?"

She sent him a narrowed glance, and then looked at the pavement some more. "Because…I'm insane and possibly a drug addict?"

"What?"

She looked up again, a flash of anger in her eyes and then, as before, back down. "I heard what you said to Ash."

He winced. But still, she shouldn't have been listening in. "You were eavesdropping."

"No, I wasn't. It just…happened. I left my purse on the front hall table. Don't ask me why, I don't why. But when I realized I'd left it there, I went back to get it. I heard you guys in the study, talking. I knew I had to go past the open door to get to the table. I knew you would see me, and I would feel foolish to have wandered off without my purse—the family idiot on the loose without a keeper. It would be just one more proof that I'm a can short of a six-pack, you know? So I hesitated. That was when I heard what you said."

Regret tugged at him. "Look, I really am sorry. I can see now I had it all wrong about you."

"Yeah, well. It seriously ticked me off at the time. But now that I've cooled off a little, I guess I have to admit that I completely get why you would think I'm out of my mind."

"So this, taking my bike, was payback?"

Still staring at the pavement, she shrugged. "In a totally wussy, pitifully ineffective sort of way, yeah."

He touched her strong little chin with his finger, guiding it up so that she was looking at him again. "We can call it even from here. Start fresh. How 'bout that?"

She made a disbelieving sound. "You sure you don't want to have me arrested?"

He held her gaze. "It's tempting, but I'll pass."

"Maybe a little time in jail would do me good," she said half-jokingly, mocking herself.

And suddenly, he wanted to shake her. She didn't have a clue about what happened behind bars.

His exasperation must have shown on his face. Her eyes widened. "Yikes. What did I say this time?"

Gruffly, he advised, "You don't want to go to jail. Take my word on that."

"Uh. Okay."

He gentled his tone. "So, you think you can drive Ash's Mercedes back to the house without running into anything?"

She hung her head again. "I could. If I could only find my way there."

He understood. "You're lost."

"Oh, yeah. In more ways than one."

He felt a surge of something that could only be called protectiveness. It surprised him. He wasn't the protective type. "Here." He took her small, soft hand, turned it over and put Ash's keys in it. "You're gonna be fine."

"Oh, I hope so."

"Just follow me."

* * *

Marnie felt a little better about everything as she followed Jericho through the dark, quiet streets of Tessa's neighborhood. Her very, very bad day was looking up a little.

Yeah, she'd let her whacked-out emotional state get the better of her and screwed up royally, stealing Jericho's bike like that. But somehow, it had worked out all right. She even had a strange feeling she might end up calling Jericho a friend.

Who would have guessed that might happen?

Life was no rose garden. But it could surprise you in a good way now and then.

Even in the dark, she recognized Tessa's street when they reached it. And she wasn't far behind when Jericho turned his bike into the driveway beside Tessa's house.

Tessa and Ash were waiting on the front step. Ash had his arm around her and she huddled close to him. The headlights of the Mercedes swept over them and Marnie saw that her sister's face was pale and drawn with worry.

Way to go, Jones.

Guilt tightened her stomach and made her feel crappy all over again. She really needed to get her act together. Making Tessa suffer for her erratic behavior was not the way to treat her loyal, generous, loving big sister. Tessa would do anything for her and she knew it. She needed to start showing a little consideration and respect.

Things got worse in the house. Ash and Tessa were there in the kitchen when Marnie and Jericho came in through the glass doors.

"Marnie!" Tessa's relief was painfully evident. "I'm so glad you're all right…." She started to come to her.

Ash held her back with a hand on her shoulder. His blue eyes were dark with fury. Marnie realized she'd never seen him angry before. But he was now—angry at *her*. "What is the matter with you? You had your sister scared to death."

"Ash, don't…" Tessa gave him a pleading look. "It's okay. *She's* okay."

Ash was not pacified. He pinned Marnie with an unforgiving glare. "You're family. That means you're welcome in this house. But you damn well better not pull any more stunts like this one tonight, or there is going to be big trouble between you and me."

Marnie felt his harsh words like blows. They were true words. And that made them hurt all the more. She opened her mouth to say she was so sorry and she would never do anything like that again.

But Tessa spoke first, her gentle voice soothing. "Ash. Come on." She turned to Marnie, her eyes moist with tears. "He worries about me. Please don't take offense."

Marnie let out a cry. "I don't. Of course, I don't. He's absolutely right."

Ash nodded. "You better believe I am."

Jericho stepped in then. "Come on, Ash. Dial it back. She knows she did wrong."

Ash shifted his furious gaze to his brother. "What? Now *you're* defending her? What's up with that?"

Marnie cleared her throat. "We, um, we came to an understanding, Jericho and me. He still thinks I'm weird—but not crazy or on drugs."

Jericho explained, "She overheard us talking in the study."

"Talking about what?" Tessa demanded.

Ash answered reluctantly, "Jericho was saying that maybe she needed professional help."

Jericho snorted. "I wasn't nearly that diplomatic about it."

"Oh, no…" Tessa stared at her pityingly.

Marnie shrugged and looked down at the floor. Since Jericho had caught up with her on his bike, she'd done a lot of looking down. "I did overhear what Jericho said. And I *was* a little crazy. But I'm pulling it together, as of now." She raised her head, straightened her spine, and made herself meet her brother-in-law's still-angry gaze. "I'm past the nervous breakdown phase. I swear I am."

Ash gave her a long once-over. Finally, he nodded. "Well, all right, then. Sorry for jumping down your throat." He pulled Tessa closer and pressed a kiss to her temple.

She nudged him in the side. "You went a little overboard, you know?"

"Yeah," Ash admitted. "Maybe. But I don't like to see you freaked out, especially now, with the baby coming."

Marnie wondered if she'd heard right. "Uh. The baby?"

Jericho let out a low chuckle.

Tessa sighed.

Ash's brows drew together. "You didn't tell her."

Tessa sent him a weary glance. "I was waiting till she at least had a good night's sleep. But so much for that."

Marnie groaned. "That's right. You didn't have even

one margarita, just to be sociable. And no wine. Only sparkling water. Am I oblivious or what?"

Tessa eased out of Ash's protective embrace. "You have a lot on your mind."

Jericho said, "Hey, Ash. Walk me out."

Marnie sent him a grateful look. "Thanks, Jericho. For everything."

"Later." One corner of his mouth twitched in what could almost be called a smile as he turned again for the French doors.

When the men were gone and the sisters were alone, Marnie grabbed Tessa in a long, tight hug. "I can hardly believe it. A baby. My sister's having a baby…." She took Tessa by the shoulders and held her away enough to look up into her sweet face. "When are you due?"

"Late October."

"You're going to be an amazing mother, you know that?"

Tessa's cheeks flushed. It was good to see some color back in them. "I'm going to give it my best shot."

"I'm so sorry I scared you. Never, ever again."

Tessa's eyes gleamed. "Well, at least if you could try and wait until after the baby's born…"

"It's a promise." She caught both of Tessa's hands. "You were always on my side—well, except when we were little. Then you tried to run my life."

Tessa looked suddenly prim. It was a look she used to wear a lot when she was a kid, back when Marnie would constantly razz her, calling her Saint Teresa. "You were a wild child," Tessa said. "You used to swear like a sailor on shore leave, remember? And you were always running away, freaking everybody out...."

Marnie felt her shoulders slump. "Looks like I'm up to my old tricks, huh? Only minus the wild part. Somewhere I lost track of that—of my wild side. Lately, I'm about as wild as a stale slice of white bread."

Tessa pulled her close again, whispered, "You're still wild at heart. You know you are."

"Oh, yeah, right."

"You are."

Marnie couldn't help asking, hopefully, "You think?"

"I *know*." Outside, Jericho's chopper roared to life. The sisters were quiet as the rumbling moved along the driveway and then faded away down the street. Then Tessa spoke again. "I'm so glad you and Jericho seem to have worked out your differences."

"I hated him at first."

"No kidding."

"But you know, I can see now that he's an okay guy after all. A really good guy, actually."

"He's got a lot of heart. And in the past few years, he's turned his life around."

Marnie wondered what exactly that meant.

But before she could ask Tessa about it, Ash came in. Marnie apologized again for everything.

Ash said he wanted to let bygones be bygones. "I'm glad you came to us. And I meant it when I said you're welcome to stay as long as you want to."

Marnie told them good night and went back to the guesthouse, where she drew a bath and sank gratefully into it, sighing in pleasure as she let the hot water ease all her tensions away.

Things could be worse, she was thinking. And then she laughed at her own sudden optimism. Her life, after all, was still a great big mess. But somehow, she felt better about it.

It wasn't even forty-eight hours since the breakup, but she was already beginning to see that her relationship with Mark really hadn't been that good for her. In the years they were together, she had slowly relinquished her life to him, until she lived in his shadow.

His friends became her friends. His world, hers. He had a big trust fund set up for him by his dad. And he also made a lot more money than she ever would. It had seemed like a good idea at the time, to just stop working, to let him support her. After all, her jobs never brought in much anyway.

Without Mark to pay the bills, she had almost nothing to call her own.

But there was a bright side. All of a sudden, she was nobody's shadow. She'd stepped into the light. She could see her life clearly now. Too bad what she saw wasn't all that great.

Mark had offered her money "to hold her over," when he told her they were through. She had proudly refused him, which had seemed really noble at the time—but was actually kind of stupid, when you got right down to it. Bottom line, she was on her own with five hundred dollars in her checking account. She had two years of junior college and a hodgepodge of subsistence-level work experience to recommend her to a prospective employer.

But she could get crazy all over again if she started dwelling on her chances of finding a decent job with her minimal skills in a not-so-great economy. She closed her eyes and let her body float in the cooling bathwater and tried to turn her wayward mind to soothing things.

For some reason, her thoughts drifted to Jericho. She could see him now, behind the dark screen of her shuttered eyelids, in the hard glare of the Mercedes' headlights, when he caught up with her on his bike.

He'd held out his arms to her.

It was the last thing she'd expected him to do.

But he *had* done it.

And somehow, that moment—when his big, tattooed arms closed around her—that was the turning point. That was when she knew: in time, she was going to be all right.

The world had simple kindness in it after all. How strange that a big, scary biker guy like Jericho Bravo had ended up being the one to make her see that.

Chapter Three

"Are you *sure* you don't mind if I stay a few weeks?" Marnie asked the next day.

It was after nine and Ash had gone to work. Marnie and Tessa were sitting at the table in the kitchen, the morning sun pouring in through the glass panes of the French doors, Tessa with a cup of herbal tea and Marnie with her third mug of coffee. Mona Lou, the bulldog, was curled up in her doggy bed nearby.

Tessa said, "The guesthouse is yours for as long as you want it. And Ash and I discussed it some more, last night after you left and we—"

"Don't tell me. He said he wished I would go away and never come back, but since he'd told me I could stay, he felt honor-bound to stick by his word."

"Oh, stop. He said no such thing. Now, will you let me finish?"

"Sorry. Go ahead."

"Well, we were talking about your situation and we got to discussing the money thing."

Marnie shrugged. "You want me to pay rent? That's reasonable."

Tessa set her cup in the saucer with a sharp clink. "Of course not."

"Tessa, it's fair. I don't mind at all."

"You are not paying us rent."

"Tessa…"

"I don't want to hear any more about that."

"Okay, okay." Marnie put up both hands. "Since you insist, I'll be more than happy to stay in your guest-house for free. And if you weren't talking about my paying rent, then…?"

"Look. Do you need money? If you do, just say so. We would be only too happy to—"

"No. Thanks. But no, thanks."

"Don't be so proud."

"I'm not." She rethought that. "Well, okay. I am. Pride's about all I have left at this point."

"It's not a big deal," Tessa insisted. "Don't make it one. If you're planning on staying for a while, you're bound to need a little cash to tide you over. "

"I have a little cash." *Very* little cash, as a matter of fact. "Also, I'm planning to earn my way while I'm here."

Her sister gave her a disapproving look and then asked, with her mouth pinched up, "A job?"

"That's right. I'm sort of a Jane-of-all-trades, after

all. I'm sure I can find something. Did you know that I was even a short-order cook once?"

Tessa was still frowning. "You want to flip burgers?"

"I *want* a paycheck for the time I'm here."

"But...there's no need to rush into anything. Maybe you should, you know, take it easy for a week or so at least. Relax. Take some time off."

"Tessa." Marnie gave her a patient look. "You so don't get it. I've *had* time off. The past five years since I've been with Mark, I've hardly worked at all."

"But if you—"

"Tessa."

"Hmm?"

"Don't go all Saint Teresa on me. Please."

Tessa put on her most innocent expression. "I would never try to tell you what to do." As if she hadn't just done exactly that.

But Marnie didn't take offense. She knew that Tessa was only being bossy out of love. "Well." Marnie sent her sister a fond smile. "Then we understand each other."

Tessa got her pinch-mouthed look again. But at least she didn't say anything more.

Ash had left the morning paper on the table. Marnie picked it up and flipped it to the want ads. What she saw there sent a little shiver down her spine.

It also made her smile. "Speaking of jobs. What do you think of that?" Marnie set down the paper and pointed.

The ad read:

Temporary Office Manager Sought
Busy motorcycle shop: repair and custom
Familiarity with Word, Excel and general office ex-

perience required. Past experience in car or motorcycle repair a plus.
Contact Gus, San Antonio Choppers (212) 555-2873

Tessa's nod was beyond reluctant. "Yeah. So?"

"Why only temporary?"

"The woman who runs the office is going on maternity leave—and you're not thinking of going to work for Jericho, are you?"

"Why not?" Marnie laughed. "You don't think he'll hold it against me that I stole his bike, do you?"

"I didn't say that."

"But you know you were thinking it."

"You're serious. You want to work in a motorcycle shop?" Tessa couldn't believe it. But then, she'd never hung around the North Magdalene Garage in the old days, helping their dad, like Marnie used to do. To Tessa, a car was for transportation, period. And a motorcycle...well, she might admire the art and technical skill that went into Jericho's choppers, but she clearly didn't find them all that intriguing.

Marnie did. "Yeah. I think it might be interesting. And it just so happens that I have experience in car repair."

"Working for Dad, you mean."

"I also know Word and Excel. More or less. And I worked in an office. Once. Accounts payable and receivable. It was *really* boring."

Tessa sipped her tea and wore her best I-am-staying-out-of-it look.

Marnie reached across and patted her arm. "Come on. Be fair. Think about it. Jericho *is* my brother-in-law. And we're on good terms—as of now, anyway. And the job sounds kind of interesting. Plus, it's temporary and I'm looking for something temporary. It could be just what I need."

Tessa set down her cup and beamed her most beatific smile. "Did I utter a word of objection?"

"You didn't have to. I can see it all over your face."

"But did I *say* anything?"

"All right, fine. No. You didn't. You're a model of total non-bossiness."

"Thank you."

"Gus is Jericho's partner in the shop, right?"

"That's right," Tessa said. "Gus owned the shop originally. And he and Jericho go way back. He let Jericho keep his first bike there, at the shop, while he was in prison."

Marnie almost choked on her coffee. "Wait. What? Somebody went to prison?"

"I thought I told you that. Jericho used to steal cars. He would sell them to some guys who parted them out to repair shops. He got caught and did five years for grand theft auto."

"Whoa. Wow. When?"

Tessa shook her head. "I could have sworn I told you all about this."

"Tessa. When?"

"He was young. Twenty, I think. That was ten years ago. He did those five years and he's been out for about five more. But right after his release, he got arrested down in Mexico for drug dealing. Gabe got him out of that one."

Marnie remembered Gabe from the wedding—tall, well-dressed, slick. Really good-looking. "Gabe's the family lawyer, right?"

"That's right. And as it turned out, the thing in Mexico was a bad rap, a complete setup."

"Jericho wasn't really dealing?"

"No. It was just some trumped-up charge because he talked back to a policeman down there. Gabe got it thrown out."

"So that was what you meant last night, when you said that Jericho has turned his life around..." Marnie thought of the spark of fury in his eyes when she'd joked about his sending her to jail for stealing his bike. His reaction made a lot more sense now.

Tessa explained, "Ash says Jericho was always the rebel of the family, the one with no interest in doing anything his father wanted him to do, ever."

Davis. That was their father's name. Marnie vaguely remembered the older man: thick, white hair, a commanding presence, a firm handshake and icy green eyes.

Tessa frowned and ran her finger around the rim of her teacup. "Davis is trying harder now to be a...kinder man than he once was. But he's a tough character. And he was building a dynasty, you know? He wanted his boys to get good educations and come to work for the family company. He had no patience for a troubled son, and no respect for Jericho's considerable mechanical skills. Ash said his dad once yelled at Jericho that he didn't need a damn grease monkey for a son. If he wanted his car fixed, he'd take it to a shop."

"What a bastard."

Tessa sighed. "Well, yeah. Davis can be a real jerk, it's true. But as I said, he's been working on lightening up—and speaking of people's fathers..."

Marnie moaned. "Oh, no. In case you didn't notice, I've been putting that off."

Tessa had on her wise-big-sister look again. "You have to let them know what's going on."

"No, I don't."

"What if Dad or Gina calls you in Santa Barbara?"

"They'll try my cell if no one answers. And if Mark picks up in Santa Barbara, he'll tell them I'm here, safe, with you."

"Marnie." Tessa said her name and then just looked at her. In her bed in the corner, Mona Lou let out a long, sad sigh.

Marnie grumbled, "You are going to make such a good mother. You're so damn sure of what other people need to be doing."

"Call home."

Marnie said darkly, "And you *know* what will happen when I do."

Tessa broke eye contact first. "Don't worry about Grandpa."

"Easy for you to say."

"You're not calling him, you're calling Dad and Gina."

"I don't have to call him. As soon as Gina and Dad know, Grandpa will find out. He *always* finds out. And you know how he is. He'll probably drive that old wreck of a Cadillac all the way here to Texas, just to give me some advice."

"Come on, Marnie. He's over ninety. His days of driving long distances are done."

"Think again. He's Oggie Jones."

"He only does it out of love."

"Well, right now, I don't need Grandpa Oggie's special brand of love."

"Marnie. Phone home."

Making that call wasn't as bad as Marnie had expected it to be. Gina clucked over her and her dad asked her if she needed money.

Why did everyone suddenly want to give her money? It was a little insulting and a lot reassuring. They loved her, she knew that. They wanted to do what they could to make sure she was okay.

She told them to hug her half brothers, Brady and Craig, for her, and hung up feeling good that they knew what was going on. Hey, she could get lucky and they wouldn't even tell her grandfather about her situation.

Well, a girl can hope....

Next, she called her birth mother in Arkansas. That was a short conversation. Marybeth Lynch Jones Leventhaal had remarried recently and her new husband was a widower with five young children. Marybeth also ran a busy real estate business. That didn't leave her a lot of time for chatting on the phone. Marnie's mom said she loved her and to call if she needed anything.

After that, she debated whether to call San Antonio Choppers and ask for the partner, Gus. Or to ask for Jericho first?

And then she decided it would work more in her favor just to show up and apply for the job. After all, she reasoned, it would be harder to turn down a needy relative in person than it would be on the phone.

* * *

Northwest of the 410 loop, on a stretch of dusty road studded with flat-roofed strip malls and used car lots, Jericho's shop was housed in a barnlike structure of gray-painted brick.

The shop's name, San Antonio Choppers, was written big and bold above the front entrance in a sort of Gothic/heavy metal–looking script on a logo shaped like a bat—or maybe a winged shield. A high chain-link fence topped with coils of barbed wire rimmed the wide circle of parking lot that surrounded the building.

Marnie drove through the open gate and parked her Camry across a stretch of blacktop from the door, next to a Harley that looked like it had been around since World War II, with handlebars wrapped in black tape and a hand-stitched rawhide seat. Feeling a little out of place, she got out of the car, straightened her snug denim skirt and walked tall across the asphalt to the thick steel front door with the wide pane of glass on the top.

Even from outside, she could hear the muffled beat of loud music, and the scream of some metal-slicing saw. And pounding. Someone was pounding with a heavy hammer—probably on steel. There were big bikes in a row close to the door and a number of mean-looking customized antique cars as well. One of the cars bore a giant plaque across the trunk that read *Pedestrian Killer*.

Marnie refused to be daunted. She marched up to that heavy door and yanked it wide.

The music got louder, so did the pounding and the scream of sawed metal. And she was only in the office, which had a high counter, a desk and file cabinets behind it. Beyond the desk and file cabinets, there was a waist-high sliding window that ran the width of the far wall, mirroring the windows that flanked the front door. Through the glass of the far window, she could see the cavernous shop itself and the men working in there. She counted at least six lifts and a welding area back in a distant corner, and steel-railed stairs going up to another level. It seemed a pretty big operation.

On the customer side of the counter, there was sort of a makeshift gift shop setup, stacks of T-shirts and sweatshirts with the San Antonio Choppers logo, a carousel draped with keychains. She spotted hats and skullcaps bearing the shop logo, and even what looked like rolls of San Antonio Choppers wrapping paper. The display could use a little tidying. Not to mention a serious encounter with a dust rag.

Burly men in old jeans, heavy boots and T-shirts sat in chairs along the wall beneath the windows on either side of the door. Marnie felt their eyes all over her. She sent a slow smile to the left and right, just to let them all know that as far as she was concerned, looking was free.

On the far side of the counter, an enormously pregnant blonde with pouffy side ponytails and some serious facial piercings dragged herself out of the chair behind the desk. "Help you?"

Marnie stepped up to the counter. "I've come about the job—the temporary one?"

The woman braced a hand on her hip and shouted good and loud toward a shut door to her left. "Gus! Job applicant!"

The door opened. A tall, lean black man with a shaved head, chin-strap beard and a moustache pulled open the door. He stuck his finger in his ear and scowled. "You got a voice like a band saw, Desiree. I'm right here."

Desiree shrugged, flipped her blond head in Marnie's direction, and lowered herself back into the desk chair with a long sigh. She picked up a stapler and began stapling papers together.

The man came toward Marnie, his wiry brown arm extended. "I'm Gus. Gus McNair." He had a beautiful tattoo of a single rattlesnake that coiled its way down and around the smooth dark skin of his arm. The snake's head, fangs showing, red forked tongue flicking, extended beyond his wrist, over the back of his hand.

She reached across the counter and their palms met. "Marnie Jones."

Gus smiled then, a slow, appreciative smile, displaying even rows of beautiful teeth. Suddenly he looked like a movie star. He could have been anywhere from forty to sixty, his skin was so smooth, with only a few crow's feet around his eyes. And with a smile like that, a girl would find it very easy to forget that he was probably old enough to be her dad. "Come on in my office," he said.

She went around the end of the counter and followed him into the small room beyond the door, which held a cluttered desk and a couple of chairs. The single window faced the front and the cinderblock walls were one continuous collage: photos of big bikes, a couple of neon-decked clocks, examples of really fine airbrush art and line drawings of several different chopper designs.

Two pit bulls, one brown and one black, lay on either side of the desk. In unison, the dogs lifted their heads from their paws when Gus led her in. The brown one yawned. Neither got up.

Gus shut the door and folded his long frame into the chair behind the cluttered desk. He indicated the paint-spattered metal chair across from him and she sat in it, sliding her purse off her arm to the floor.

"Here." He produced an application from the pile of stuff on the desk, and then took a pen from the desk drawer and gave her that as well. "Clear off a space on your side and fill it out. Then we'll talk." With that, he put his feet up on the corner of the desk, leaned back, linked his long-fingered hands on his stomach and shut his eyes.

Marnie stared at him for a moment, bemused. Was he asleep?

"Go on, fill it out," he said, without opening his eyes.

So she did, giving Tessa's address as her residence and her own cell for a phone number. In the section for previous employment, she put down the payables/receivables job and her father's garage, lying about the dates a little, extending the time she'd worked at both.

"Done?" He opened his eyes and sat up.

She handed the form across the desk to him.

He leaned back again, hoisted his boots to the desk and stroked his neatly trimmed silver-gray beard as he read. "What area code's your cell?"

"Santa Barbara."

"How long you been in town?"

"Since yesterday."

He slanted her a look. His eyes were a brown so deep they appeared black. They were kind eyes, but she saw doubts in them and had the sinking feeling he wasn't going to hire her. "This is an Olmos Park address. You got a house in Olmos Park, Marnie Jones?" Meaning what did she need with a temporary job at a motorcycle shop if she lived in a wealthy neighborhood?

"It's my sister's house. I'm staying with her."

"The job is for six weeks, while Desiree's having that baby you might have noticed she's about to drop any minute."

"Six weeks would be great. I'm kind of…open-ended, at the moment."

He chuckled, a deep, smooth-as-velvet sound. "Open-ended, huh?"

"Yes."

"Say you decide to head on back to Cali before the six weeks are up. Where does that leave me?"

"But I won't. That wouldn't be right. If you hire me, I'm here for as long as I say I'll be here."

He tipped his shiny, smooth head and studied her. "You telling me I can count on you?"

"Absolutely."

"You seem like a nice girl, Marnie." He definitely had that tone—the one that said he was trying to gently ease her on out the door. "But your office experience is sketchy."

She was leaning forward by then, *willing* him to hire her. Strangely, the more certain she became that he would turn her down, the more she wanted the job. "I know all the computer stuff. I learn fast. And I'm no slacker."

"Let me ask you this. You even know what a chopper *is?*"

She remembered the bikers she'd met at her dad's

garage and the things they had explained to her about their world. "I do, as a matter fact. It's a custom-built motorcycle, with radical styling, and a raked front end—longer forks at a greater angle than a standard bike."

He gave her a slow nod. "Close enough. But I still don't get it."

"Don't get what?"

"Truthfully now, you want to work here, why?"

It was a good question. And she wasn't sure she had an answer. Probably because it was a damn sight more to her liking than the hamburger place she was heading for next.

Not that she could tell Gus that. "Well, my dad owns a garage in my hometown. It's on the form there. I always liked it, helping him out, running the office for him. And, also, um…" She blew out a hard breath and brought out the big guns. "Your partner is my brother-in-law."

Gus's black Converse high-tops hit the floor. "Jericho?"

She swallowed and nodded.

"His family is rolling in green."

"So I understand."

"If you're married to one of his brothers, you don't need a temporary job here. We both know that." He was looking at her like he didn't believe a word she'd told him.

She suppressed a sigh. "But I'm not married to one of his brothers. His brother, Ash, is married to my sister."

He smiled again. Slowly. She couldn't tell whether her being family to his partner made a difference—or he continued to think she was lying through her teeth. "Well, angel. You should have said so upfront."

"Yeah. Guess so."

"You talked to Rico about this?"

"The ad said to ask for you," she offered lamely.

Gus was already on his feet. "He's in the shop. Wait right here."

He went out and she waited, eyeing the two pit bulls, both of which seemed to have forgotten she was there.

Gus returned with Jericho in no time. When he led her brother-in-law in, the room seemed cramped, dwarfed by Jericho's size and his considerable presence—and by Gus, too, who wasn't as big as Jericho, but had energy and charisma to spare.

Jericho didn't sit down. Neither did Gus. That couldn't be good.

"How you doin', Marnie?" Jericho asked.

"Hey."

"Gus tells me you're looking for temporary work."

"That's right."

With a nod, Gus clicked his tongue at the dogs. They followed him out. She was left alone with her huge brother-in-law who did not look especially thrilled to see her.

Jericho hitched a hard thigh up on the edge of Gus's desk and rested his big tattooed elbow on his knee. "Okay. It's just us. What's this about?"

She told the simple truth. "I'm staying in San Antonio for a while. And I need a job while I'm here. I looked in the want ads…and there was Gus's ad. It seemed kind of…I don't know, karmic maybe?"

"Karmic." He didn't look amused. He ran a huge hand down his face. "Look, Marnie..."

Everything about him—his voice, his glum expression, the tired way he dragged his hand down his face—it all said that this was not going to happen.

Grabbing her purse, she stood. "Okay. Getting the picture here. Karmic was a really bad word choice—because you have no intention of hiring me, no matter what I say."

He had the good grace to look pained at least. "I'm sorry."

"Don't be. Hey. I get it. Can't have someone working for you who steals the merchandise."

"It's not that. We're past that."

"Well, I thought we were."

"It's...you're kind of up in the air now, right?"

"Yeah. So?"

"Around here, we gotta have someone we can depend on to handle the front. You could decide tomorrow that you want to work things out with your boyfriend and you have to go."

"There won't be any working things out with Mark."

"You say that now."

"And I'll be saying it next week. And every week after that. He ended it with me. There's no going back."

"Maybe he'll snap out of it, realize he made a big mistake."

"Too late. I'm done."

"But Marnie, come on. You could always have a change of heart."

"How much clearer can I be about this? It's over between me and Mark. Finished. Dead with a stake to the heart. And as far as my just taking off, no. I would never do that. If I give my word that I'll be here till your regular person comes back, I'll be here."

He looked down at his boots, reminding her of last night, when *she* had been the one looking down. "Honestly. I'd like to give you a try…."

"…But you're not going to." She made her voice flat, not allowing even a trace of bitterness to creep in.

He lifted his big head and met her eyes then. "I just don't think it's a good idea."

She wanted to argue. Maybe even to yell at him, tell him loud and proud that she had really liked him for a while there last night and now she had no idea why.

But no. If he wasn't going to hire her, yelling at him wouldn't improve the situation. Plus, she was trying to act like a reasonably sane person from now on. Pitching a hissy fit wouldn't do a thing for her already-tarnished image.

It was off to Burger Paradise for her.

"All right, then," she said briskly. "I won't waste any more of your time." She stuck out her hand. He frowned at it for a moment and she felt foolish for having offered it. But then, just before she pulled it back, he engulfed it with his giant paw. "No big deal," she added, proud that she sounded so cool and unruffled. "You never know if you don't try."

"Look. If you—"

She put up the hand he wasn't holding. "Uh-uh. Leave it. No hard feelings, okay?"

Those green eyes of his seemed to look right through her. And not in a bad way. More in a kind of surprised, interested way.

His fingers were warm and rough around hers. And he'd been holding on for much too long. Gently, she pulled free. "Whoever you hire, get her to dust the gift area. You won't sell any of that stuff as long as it all looks like it needs hosing off."

He blinked. She found that kind of satisfying. "Those T-shirts and crap, you mean?"

"If you don't want to spiff up the merchandise a little, you should get rid of it. No point in doing a thing half-assed."

She turned and got out of there before he could say more.

Chapter Four

"What's the matter with you?" Gus asked Jericho as soon as Marnie left.

He'd come right back into his private office after she went out and blocked the door so that Jericho couldn't escape without telling him to step aside. Gus was looking at him the way his own father used to. Kind of bewildered and deeply annoyed, both at once.

It was a look that made Jericho want to break something. "What do you mean, what's wrong with me?" He said it quietly. Jericho always spoke softly when he found himself starting to get pissed off. "Nothing's wrong with me." He made a move toward the door. Maybe Gus would fall back.

Not a chance. "You didn't hire her." It was an accusation.

"So?" he asked rationally. Calmly. "You said yourself her experience was thin. We'll take one of the other applicants." There had been several. "And come on. You weren't going to hire her either."

"Yeah, but that was before you told me that she really is family to you."

Jericho ran a hand back over his hair. The long strands caught on his calloused fingers. "Consider this. If you wanted me to hire her, you should have said so."

"I shouldn't have *had* to say so."

Jericho reminded himself of how many ways he owed the man in front of him. A *lot* of ways. Thousands. If not for Gus, he'd probably have come to a bad end long ago.

Gus clapped him on the side of the arm, hard. "Family needs help, you give it to them. You know that."

"She say she needed help?"

"She's staying with her sister, got an out-of-state cell phone number. If she didn't need a hand up, she wouldn't be hunting for a job." Gus gave him a long, slow look of careful regard. "Something else going on here? You got a thing for her?"

"Hell, no." He said it way too fast.

Gus smiled his wide, white smile. "She does it for you. And that scares you. Scares the big, bad Jericho."

"Remind me why I'm not going to punch your lights out."

"Because you love me, man. And that wouldn't be respectful."

"She's not my type." Now, why had he said that? There had been no need to say that.

Gus chuckled. "Your type being whoever's sitting at the bar on Saturday night."

"Is that a crime? I like to keep things casual. And besides, well, come on. Look who's talkin'."

Gus refused to engage on that point. "You should be ashamed of yourself, not giving that sweet little girl the job she needs, not helping out someone who's family to you."

Okay, maybe he *was* a little bit ashamed. Maybe he should have hired her, the more he thought about it. The job wasn't exactly rocket science. And Marnie seemed like a quick study. And if she didn't work out, it was hardly a lifetime commitment. They could put up with her for six weeks. Grudgingly, he conceded, "You want to hire her, do it. It's your call anyway."

"Not anymore. You pushed me clean out of that picture when you made the decision to send her away without bothering to consult me."

"So slide on back into the picture."

"Uh-uh. It's on you now, my brother."

That night at around eight, Marnie sat in the living room of the guesthouse. She'd already washed her face and brushed her teeth. Now, all ready for bed in her favorite sleep shirt, she was watching a rerun of *Two and a Half Men,* with one bare foot up on the coffee table and cotton between her toes, carefully stroking on teal-blue glitter nail polish.

When she happened to glance up, Jericho was standing on the other side of the glass door that opened onto the backyard. She let out a tiny squeak of surprise and almost knocked the bottle of polish to the rug.

One eyebrow lifted, he rapped his knuckles on the door.

She took her time about letting him in, carefully screwing the cap back on the polish, making a big project of getting up and smoothing her long shirt down over her bare thighs. Finally, when she couldn't in good conscience make him wait any longer, she limped over to the door. That took longer than it should have because she was trying to keep her half-polished toes from getting smeared as she went.

She opened the door just wide enough to stick her head through. "What? You live to make me squeal in terror?"

His rather sexy mouth quirked just the smallest bit at one corner in his own personal version of a smile. "You gonna let me in?"

She blew out a breath. "Oh, I suppose." She turned and hobbled back to the couch, leaving it up to him to push the door the rest of the way open for himself. "I think there's a Corona in the fridge. You want one?"

"Sure."

"Go for it." She waved a hand in the direction of the kitchen and dropped to the couch again, lifting her foot back into position, the ball of it braced on the edge of the coffee table. He returned a moment later. "Have a seat," she offered, not glancing up because she was busy stroking on polish again.

He settled into a wing chair. "Hot date?"

She laughed—though it came out as more like a snort. "Yeah. It's one wild Friday night for me. A bath, a pedicure and at least eight hours' sleep—I didn't hear your bike."

"I brought one of the whips and parked on the street."

"Whips…as in those custom cars I saw parked around the shop?"

"That's right. You find a job?"

"You bet."

"Where?"

She waved the polish brush airily. "It's a very glamorous position and I don't feel like going into it right now."

"Waitressing?"

"Even better. Carhopping. At Sonic."

"You get good tips doing that?"

"I'm certainly going to find out." She glanced his way then.

He'd kind of slouched down in the chair and he watched her through brooding eyes. "Gus liked you."

She laughed again. "Right. I knew that by the way he jumped at the chance to hire me."

"He did like you. And he's a good man. The best there is. A good judge of people."

In spite of her intention to keep things light and slightly sarcastic, she felt pleased. And she let it show in her voice. "I believe that. I would guess not a lot gets past him."

"And he can fix any broken-down piece of junk you might wheel into the shop."

She finished one foot, so she put it down and the other one up and began poking fresh cotton balls into place between that set of toes. When she looked over at him, she caught him staring at her bare legs.

He refused to pretend he hadn't been, only slowly raised his gaze to meet hers. She saw green fire in those eyes of his and a flare of heat sizzled through her.

She liked it, the heat. It was soothing to her recently battered ego. To know that a man—especially a big, muscled manly man like Jericho, a man with testoster-one to spare—found her attractive. Lately, she'd begun to wonder. With Mark, well, it had never been about sex. And in the past year or so…

Uh-uh. She wasn't going back there. All that was behind her now.

Jericho spoke again. "You know that old movie, *Easy Rider?*"

"Of course. I always admired that chopper Peter Fonda rode, with the gas tank painted like the American flag?"

"That bike?"

"Yeah?"

"A black man built that bike."

"I didn't know that."

He shrugged, a slight lift of one ginormous shoulder. "We're not all into that Aryan Brotherhood crap, no matter the rap we get."

"I know." She spoke softly. They shared a long look.

Then he said, "Gus and me talked. He really got on me for not hiring you. He said I should be ashamed of myself. And you know what? I think I agree with him."

She felt gratified—and she couldn't help teasing, "Oh, like you want to hire me out of pity now?"

"Not pity." He looked at her levelly. "And you do need a job."

"I have a job."

"But we'll pay more. And we'll offer…more of a challenge, more variety."

"At Sonic, I'll get tips."

He laughed at that, a low, rough, pleasing sound. And then he grew serious. "Come to work for SA Choppers, Marnie."

"You mean it? You really have rethought this and my working there is what *you* want, that you're not just doing it because Gus shamed you into it, or because you feel you should?"

"I've rethought it. And I am good with it. I...want it."

She slanted him a glance. "If I made you, would you beg?"

He answered gruffly. "How 'bout this? You don't make me beg—but you can tell everyone I did."

Marnie started Monday morning. The plan was that she would get a few days with Desiree, to learn the ropes before she had to handle everything on her own.

But Desiree went into labor Saturday night and had a baby girl Sunday morning. So Gus got the job of walking Marnie through her duties, which included everything from keeping the coffee made through invoicing and manning the cash register to answering the phones. She was also in charge of the gift area, a duty she took on with glee.

The way she saw it, if the merchandise was displayed attractively and she put a little effort into guiding the customers' interest that way, the shop could clean up. There was a serious markup on stuff like T-shirts and key chains. Marnie knew this because Tessa had owned a gift shop in North Magdalene before she married Ash. Tessa sold a lot of theme T-shirts—T-shirts with mountain-biking logos, T-shirts with a California theme, Gold Country T-shirts. She'd always said she made a mint on them.

Monday at lunch, Gus had one of the shop guys

handle the front counter for an hour and took Marnie to a coffee shop down the street. She told him about her plans for the gift area.

He said she should go for it. "Anything that brings in more revenue is a good thing as far as I'm concerned. You're a real go-getter, aren't you, angel? Keep it up."

She returned his beautiful smile. "I plan to." She asked him about the pit bulls.

He told her their names were Chichi and Dave. "Chichi's the brown one."

"They are the calmest, sleepiest pit bulls I've ever seen."

Gus shrugged. "They are, aren't they? I like a sleepy, good-natured dog."

That first week, she was too busy getting to know the invoicing system and dealing with customers to do much about the condition of the front area. She hardly saw Jericho. He was putting in long hours on the chopper for Ash's charity event. But Gus took her to lunch every day.

She wanted to know everything about the shop.

Gus was only too happy to enlighten her. He explained that he'd built a chopper or two himself and had been building bikes as a sideline, a passion, since he was a kid. But Jericho was the main designer, the force behind making the shop more about building bikes than repairing them. Gus said Jericho had real genius, that when you build choppers, you have to be an artist and an engineer, a welder, an inspired fabricator and a damn good mechanic. Jericho was all those things, a natural talent who, after a rough start in life, worked hard at what he did and kept getting better at it.

When Gus asked her about herself, about her life before she'd come to SA, she told him. About her hometown, about her family, about Mark and how his dumping her had been the force behind her ending up at SA Choppers for the next six weeks. Gus listened to her the way he did everything: with a kind of complete, yet relaxed, attention.

She liked Gus a lot. He was a wise man in so many ways. He reminded her a little of her Grandpa Oggie. Except he was younger, a lot nicer to look at and not nearly so aggravating.

The job included a half day on Saturday. But Sunday was all hers. Ash and Tessa were going out to the family ranch, Bravo Ridge, to spend the afternoon and have Sunday dinner. They invited Marnie.

She tried to back out of it, partly because it would be nice to have the day to herself after the busy workweek. But also because it didn't feel right that Tessa and Ash had to drag her along everywhere they went.

But they insisted that it was a family thing and they really wanted her to come. Plus, she had backed out the Sunday before, Easter Sunday. She supposed it was about time she went.

Bravo Ridge, on the southwestern edge of the Hill Country, was a working horse ranch.

Luke, third-born of the family, lived there full-time and ran the place. The ranch house was big and white and imposing. Marnie thought it looked like something Thomas Jefferson might have lived in, with giant white pillars along the front verandah. In the back, there were gardens and acres of green lawn and an Olympic-size swimming pool.

That day, Marnie met Luke's wife, Mercy, and their eleven-month-old son, Lucas, who was a big kid, already walking, with his mother's black hair. The Bravo parents, Davis and Aleta, were there, too. Aleta greeted Marnie with a warm hug and said how glad she was to see her again.

From Davis, she got a handshake and a "Welcome to Bravo Ridge."

Jericho arrived at a little after three, which kind of surprised her. She'd assumed from the things Tessa had said about him that he didn't show up at family get-togethers very often.

When he got there, they were in the kitchen, all the women—Aleta, Mercy, Tessa and Marnie. The men had gone out to the stables to check out some horse or something. Even little Lucas went, toddling along, holding on to his father's thumb.

"Jericho." Aleta said his name in a pleased tone when he appeared in the kitchen doorway. She rushed over to him and went on tiptoe to kiss him.

Marnie was staring at him with her mouth open. She shut it, fast, when his mother stepped back and those jade eyes of his found hers. "What?" He was glaring.

She let out a short, embarrassed laugh. "It's just, well, you cut your hair."

"It looks good," said Tessa. Mercy and Aleta agreed.

"Yeah. Great," Marnie said. "Really." There was maybe an inch or two left now and it had a slight curl, which was definitely attractive.

"Right." He spoke in that quiet, ironic tone that told her he didn't believe her—or any of them.

Marnie knew she should let it go, but she didn't. "It's just a surprise, that's all. And it was pretty long. I mean, that must have been a big decision…" Her voice trailed off as he rubbed the back of his neck and she thought he was a little embarrassed to have them all looking at him, discussing his haircut. She found his self-consciousness endearing, for some reason.

"Summer's coming," he muttered. "It sticks to my neck."

The others agreed it was probably much cooler this way.

He laughed, shaking his head, and let his big arm drop to his side. "You play pool?"

She realized he was asking her. "Uh. Sure."

"Come on back to the game room."

The other women urged her to go, so she followed him to a big room with a wood-beam ceiling, a wet bar in one corner and stuffed animal heads decorating the walls. There were several game tables—for chess, checkers and poker. And a beautiful pool table with intricately carved legs.

"My grandfather had this table custom made," he said, "back in the sixties. Cost a mint even then. Grandpa James was a son of a bitch, a real mean character. He liked to make money. And to spend it."

"Tessa told me that *he* had seven sons, too. Like your dad."

"That's right. They all got the hell away as soon as they were old enough to be on their own. Except my dad. He was first-born, as tough and mean as Grandpa

James, and determined to stick it out. He got everything—the ranch, the money, the business—when Grandpa died. And he's made even more on top of what he inherited."

"He seemed very nice today, your father."

Jericho grunted. "He had his come-to-Jesus moment last year. My mom left him. She made him clean up his act in terms of being such an SOB before she would take him back."

"Tessa said he was trying to change, to be a kinder person. She also mentioned that he was especially hard on you, when you were growing up."

Quickly and expertly, he racked the balls. "Well, maybe he had a reason. I was a tough-ass, badmouth kid. I never met a rule I couldn't break—or an authority I didn't mess with, just for the fun of it." He broke. Two solids dropped. He moved around the table for his next shot.

"Tessa said that you used to steal cars and that you went to prison for it."

He sent her a sideways look as he bent over the table. "That's right. And I like your sister, but she talks too much."

"Jericho. You've got sisters. You ought to know by now that talking too much is what we do."

Another ball dropped. He straightened and indicated the rack of pool cues on the wall. "You need to choose your weapon."

They played several games. He was really good. But she ran the table more than once. She found herself getting used to his haircut, learning to like it. It made him look even manlier than before—if that was possible. And the sight of him bending over that pool table, sighting down his cue, one powerful tattooed arm out straight, green eyes focused, sharp as a bird of prey…well, that was really something to see. It made her heart beat faster, made her feel a little breathless, truth be told.

The second time she won, he got them each a beer and they sat on the long rawhide couch together, between the chess table and the one with the poker chips on it.

She told him how she'd learned to play pool, in her family's bar at home, The Hole in the Wall. "I learned to play poker at The Hole in the Wall, too," she said. "My grandpa owned that bar for decades. And then my Uncle Jared and Aunt Eden took it over. Aunt Eden opened a restaurant next door."

He was watching her, his gaze moving from her mouth to her eyes and back again. She liked it—liked his gaze on her. It made her feel kind of warm and lazy. Kind of excited and content, both at the same time.

And then he brought up SA Choppers. "The job working out for you?"

She gave an eager nod. "I love it. I really do."

He smiled. "Your eyes are shining."

She laughed. "It's just…I don't know. It's got lots of variety. There's never a dull moment. The customers are great, lots of attitude, you know? But in a good way."

He was watching her mouth again. "You like attitude?"

"Well, I grew up with a lot of attitude around me. The men in my family are kind of famous for their wild partying ways. They liked to drink to excess, play cards for high stakes—and maybe enjoy a nice bar fight to cap off the night. My dad and his brothers settled down eventually. But my two younger brothers and my male cousins are all showing promise of being just as bad and out of control as my dad and my uncles ever were."

He lifted a hand. She thought he was going to touch her and she realized she wanted him to. But then he just shifted his beer to that hand and drank. "You smile when you talk about them."

"Yeah. It's easy to appreciate them from eighteen hundred miles away—and we were talking about my job at SA Choppers.…"

"That's right. We were."

"I think I can build the gift shop area into a profitable sideline. I read somewhere that sixty percent of the revenue at West Coast Choppers comes from the gift shop they have in front—and yeah, I know, West Coast Choppers has Jesse James and he's famous and all, but you've got quite the reputation yourself. I really think you should take advantage of the merchandising opportunity."

He chuckled. "Well, you've got five weeks left to show us how we've been missing the boat."

"That's what Gus says, more or less. As soon as I'm on top of the basic stuff, he told me the gift area is mine."

"You and Gus…I noticed you been going to lunch together."

She didn't like his tone and she spoke sharply in return. "What? Something wrong with that?"

He looked at her for a long, slow moment. And then he shrugged. "It's just…the women love him. And he loves women. *All* women. I've known him half my life.

He was married once, for over twenty years. I knew his wife, Karen, a really great woman. He never looked at another lady while she was alive."

Marnie's throat felt dry. She swallowed. "She died?"

He nodded. "Of cancer."

"When?"

"Eight years ago."

"That's awful."

"Yeah. He really loved her and they were happy and since her, he never gets serious about anyone. It's all just good times for him."

She stared. "You're…you're *warning* me? About Gus?"

"Don't play it like you're surprised."

"I'm not playing it. I *am* surprised."

"You and him had lunch together every day last week."

"We work together. He's teaching me the job."

"And that's all he's teaching you?" He was scoffing at her.

She just didn't get it. "Yeah. Really, Jericho. I like him. He likes me. We work together. And I don't see why it's such a big deal to you." She was starting to get pissed off at him. And she didn't want that, didn't want them on bad terms again when they seemed to have reached a kind of peace between them. She took a deep breath and purposely gentled her tone. "Gus is…wise, you know? I like him a lot. But we're just friends, seriously. Nothing more."

His eyes were cold, unbelieving. "You say that."

"Yeah. Because it's true."

"Well. Okay." He seemed doubtful, but ready to let it go.

Her curiosity got the better of her. "Does Gus have any kids?"

He drank from his beer, tipping his big head back, his throat working as he swallowed. Finally, he looked at her again. "No."

"What? Suddenly it's all a big secret?"

"Gus doesn't like to talk about his wife or the kids they never had."

"Ho-kay. So I'm not asking him, I'm asking you."

"Look. Wake up. Karen McNair is not the point here."

She sat back away from him. "Jericho. Sheesh. Sorry."

He eased off the hostility. A little. "I just don't want you to get hurt. Seems to me you been through enough lately."

"Gus is not going to hurt me. I don't know why you keep insisting that he will."

"Well, hey. It's your life." He stood. "We should go. I smell dinner."

And that was it, end of convo. She followed him back down the hall to join the others, wondering about the wife Gus had loved and lost, the kids he'd never had.

And also why, every time she and Jericho made peace, something new happened to get one of them ticked off at the other again.

Monday, Gus and Marnie had lunch together, same as every day the week before. The whole time they sat in the coffee shop, Marnie longed to ask him about the things Jericho had revealed the day before.

But Jericho had said that Gus didn't like to talk

about his wife. So Marnie kept her nosy personal questions to herself.

Back at work, Gus let her handle the job on her own. It was fine. The rest of the day went off without a hitch. She had a great time, dealing with the customers and also joking around with the guys from the shop whenever they came up to the front to talk to a customer or clarify an item on an invoice.

By Tuesday, Marnie was ready to spiff the place up a notch. Desiree, she had learned, was a good worker, but not real anal about the way things looked or the mess on her desk. Marnie liked a tidier work space. Between customers, when the phone wasn't ringing, she gave the gift area a thorough cleaning and then rearranged it to be more enticing. After lunch with Gus, she cleaned out Desiree's desk and filed everything that wasn't nailed down.

And every time she rang up a sale, she asked if the customer wanted anything from the gift shop before she ran the total. She really did some selling using that approach. Not so much if the customer was alone, but girlfriends and kids ate it up. They all wanted an SA Choppers skullcap or sweatshirt. At the rate she was selling, she was going to need new merchandise long before Desiree's return. What they had back in the storeroom wouldn't last very long.

When she and Gus went to lunch that Wednesday, she proposed ordering from other sources. She explained that Tessa had some really good connections in California for getting logo clothing and such.

Gently, he reminded her, "It's only for six weeks, angel. Don't go getting too invested."

She knew he was right. Still, she felt sort of crestfallen. It was important to her, to make a difference while she was at SA Choppers. Even if it was only to help them see that they were ignoring a potential gold mine in the merchandising area.

Her disappointment must have shown on her face because he relented. "Tell you what. You look into it, work up some figures. Then we'll talk."

She tapped her plastic glass of iced tea against his Pepsi. "You're going to be so glad you gave me the go-ahead on this. I promise you, Gus."

"Angel, if it makes you happy, it tickles me pink."

Jericho had had enough.

He'd tried to warn Marnie about getting so involved with Gus and she'd blown him off, given him the innocent eyes, the oh-don't-worry-we're-just-good-friends crap.

Just good friends.

Right. He didn't believe it. Damn it, Gus ought to know better. The woman was family and she was just coming off a major heartbreak. She didn't need another guy to take advantage of her weakened state.

He was going to have to deal with Gus on this, which was why he was waiting up in front when she and Gus got back from lunch Wednesday.

"Got a minute?" he asked his partner when the two of them came in, laughing over some private joke or other.

Marnie slanted him a questioning look, which Jericho was careful to ignore as Gus signaled him into the front office. Once they were both in there, alone with Chichi and Dave, Gus shut the door and went around the desk, stepping over Chichi, to drop into his chair. "All right. Talk to me."

Easy for Gus to say. But now Jericho was in here, staring across the piled-high desk at the man he would trust with his life and the lives of everyone who mattered to him, he hardly knew where to begin.

Eventually, Gus tried again. "Rico, if you got a problem, we can't deal with it unless you tell me what it is."

Jericho yanked the spare chair around and sat in it backward. "It's like this. You been to lunch with Marnie every day since she started working here. What's that about?"

Gus sat very still. In the silence of the small room, the sounds from the shop—loud music and louder machines—seemed to swell in volume.

And then the older man threw back his shiny head and let out a long, rich, rolling laugh.

Jericho resisted the urge to leap free of the chair, power across the messy desk and grab his longtime friend and mentor—his salvation, really—by the throat. If Gus had been anybody else...

But he wasn't.

Finally, Gus said, "You're some kind of fool, Rico. But you're not a stupid fool. Not anymore. Right?"

Jericho got the reference. Back in the day when trouble was his middle name, Gus would always say to him, *You're a good kid deep down, Rico. But when you going to get the stupid out of your system?* And when Jericho got out of prison and Gus gave him a job, the older man had asked, *So is this it? The end of your stupid phase?*

He had sworn that it was.

"No," Jericho said with dangerous mildness. "I'm not a stupid fool. Just a fool, period. I guess. Because I don't know what you're talking about."

A silence. Then, disbelieving, "You don't know."

"No, Gus. I don't."

"I say you do. Somewhere inside that thick head of yours, you know exactly what's going on here." Gus paused. And then he chuckled. "You're not going to admit it, are you?" He leveled that dark gaze straight at Jericho. "I'm not the threat to that sweet girl's tender heart, not the one you're worried is going to hurt her. You know that as well as I do. You need to get over yourself, man. She's a grown woman and capable of making a choice for herself. Just make your move. Let her take it from there. My bet is you won't be disappointed. She likes you, too."

"My move."

"That's what I said."

"But I'm not—"

"What? Interested? You know you are. *Good* enough? Sure, you are. Just do it. Ask her out. If she says yes, take it one day at a time. That's how all important things happen, Rico. One damn day at a time."

Chapter Five

Marnie didn't know what Jericho and Gus were talking about, locked up together in Gus's office like that. But she had a feeling it probably wasn't anything good. Jericho had looked so grim before he followed Gus in there. And Gus hadn't seemed all that happy either.

But then, after maybe five minutes, Jericho came out.

She turned from the counter, asked softly, "What's going on?"

And he pretended he didn't hear her, just brushed right on by her and through the door into the shop. Really, he could be so aggravating sometimes.

Later, when Gus came out with the dogs at his heels, he told her not to worry. "Everything is fine, angel. Just fine."

She didn't believe him. Something weird was going on. She could feel it.

At three, Gus relieved her for her afternoon break. She got a pink lemonade from the vending machine and went outside to sit on the stone bench beneath a scraggly Chinese pistache tree on the edge of the parking lot. It was that time of year, clear skies and mild temperatures. Nice to be outside, in the dappled shade of a tree, even a pitiful-looking one.

She admired the various whips in the lot—an early-fifties Chevy, chopped low, painted metal-flake yellow; an ancient Ford pickup with a giant front grill of shiny chrome, the body painted metallic watermelon red. Some of the guys really put a lot of time into their rides.

Jericho was halfway across the parking lot before she realized he was coming her way. She suddenly felt nervous, just watching him come toward her. His square jaw was set and his eyes…she couldn't read the look in them.

A shiver of fear went through her. She had to resist the sudden, silly urge to jump up and take off at a run around the perimeter of the lot, headed for the open gate.

He came and stood above her, his big body blocking the shop and most of the parking lot. "Marnie." He stared down at her, a muscle twitching his jaw, his mouth kind of set.

Was he mad at her for some reason? Sheesh. She really could not figure him out.

She lifted her lemonade and took a long, cool sip before she answered him, stalling partly to take the edge off her strange nervousness. And partly to show him he didn't scare her. She set the lemonade down on the bench hard enough that the plastic bottle made a thwack of sound. "What?"

He swore then, under his breath. "Look. Would you…?" He seemed to run out of words.

"What?" she asked again.

He did more swearing. "I know this is a really bad idea and probably the last thing you want to deal with right now."

She got up and stood facing him. "Jericho."

"Yeah?"

"I have no clue what you're talking about."

He lifted one giant, muscled arm and rubbed the back of his neck. "I'm not really sure what I'm talking about either."

That struck her as funny for some reason. Or maybe it was just that she needed a way to ease the weird tension between them. She laughed.

He let his arm drop to his side and gaped at her. "You think this is funny?"

She was still laughing. It seemed to get funnier and funnier. She shook her head, pointed at him, laughed some more.

That was when he reached out and grabbed her by the arms. He did it gently. But the sudden move surprised her nonetheless.

She stopped laughing. She stared up into his leaf-green eyes. She heard herself whisper, "Jericho…"

And then she understood. Out of nowhere, it all fell into place for her.

He…liked her. In *that* way. He wanted her.

Wanted *her*, specifically.

The very idea of that seemed completely impossible—and yet so deeply satisfying, both at the same time.

Because, well, she wanted him, too. She hadn't realized it until that moment, when he grabbed her and looked down into her eyes and everything suddenly shifted, when she saw that all of it, this edgy thing between them, made the most amazing kind of sense.

He was just what she needed in her life right now. Danger and heat and a certain raw tenderness.

She surged up on tiptoe as he lowered his head.

And then they were kissing. Wildly. Passionately. His tongue was in her mouth and his huge, hard arms engulfed her. It was so good. She hadn't felt this hot and bothered since…

Well, come to think of it, she'd *never* felt this hot and bothered. Maybe in high school, but that was so long ago. Who remembered? She and Mark had been together since dirt and what she had with him just wasn't about sex. They were companions, best friends forever, not passionate lovers.

Mark…

She thought his name, felt the ache of loss in her heart, and then rejected it. She concentrated on this, now. This was everything she hadn't even known she was missing. It was so good. The way Jericho's hard chest crushed her breasts, the taste of his mouth, the scent of his skin.

He smelled hot, like a fire. A fire burning, for her.

But then, he pulled back. Just like that, out of nowhere, he put her away from him. "I'm sorry," he said in that low, rough rumble that sang along her nerves, a tune that seemed to have been written for her and her alone.

Another burst of laughter escaped her. "Sorry? Don't be sorry. Just shut up and do that again."

And for once, he didn't argue. With a low groan, he yanked her back against him and covered her mouth with his.

They kissed for a decade. And she could have gone on kissing him for another decade more.

But they'd been spotted. There were whistles and catcalls and clapping coming from over by the door to the shop.

Jericho let her go. She really wished he hadn't, but she didn't argue that time. He turned to the guys who had gathered at the front entrance and waved an arm at them. "Okay. Knock it off. Show's over."

There was one more loud, long whistle, and they dispersed.

Jericho turned back to her. "We should talk."

We should do a whole lot more than talk. "Tonight," she said. "The guesthouse. Eight."

"I'll be there." He touched the side of her face, then. And he gazed into her eyes again. And she thought she would lose it, right there, just come all over herself from the touch of his hand on her cheek and the sizzling heat in those eyes of his.

Then he turned and left. Her knees felt wobbly. She sank back to the bench and watched him walk away from her.

She had dinner that night in the main house with Tessa and Ash. Tessa asked her if something was bothering her.

"Not a thing. Why?"

"I don't know. You seem kind of preoccupied."

Marnie lied and said she wasn't. But she had to force herself to eat the really excellent prime rib. Her mind wasn't on food that evening.

More than once, she caught herself in the act of lifting her fingers to her lips. She kept remembering the feel of Jericho's kiss. It seemed almost as if the press of his mouth on hers had left her lips tingling, a slightly hot tingling. Almost like burning.

Tessa had made Boston cream pie—which was actually yellow cake with egg custard filling and bittersweet chocolate icing on top—for dessert. The recipe was Gina's, one she used to make for them when they were kids. Marnie knew her sister had prepared the dessert with her in mind. So she lingered at the table, eating the cake, listening to Tessa and Ash talk about their plans for the baby's room.

It was quarter of eight when she finally got away. She took a quick shower, put on a white silk wraparound robe that showed more than it covered, and pulled back the blankets on the bed. She felt absolutely no coyness about what she was doing.

She wanted to have sex with Jericho. And she intended to. That night.

He arrived right on time, appearing as he had that other night, at the glass door that faced the main house. When she let him in, she could see that his hair was damp from a shower. She could smell the clean, moist scent of his skin. And the heat. Even after a shower, to her, he smelled of heat. Like forged metal, so hot it glowed red.

She closed the curtains and flipped the blinds inside

the glass of the door to the shut position, blocking out the view of the pool and the main house beyond. And also eliminating the possibility that her sister might glance out the kitchen window and see her climbing Jericho like a tree.

When she turned back from the door, he put his hand on her shoulder, clasping. The simple touch made her whole body ache with yearning. She tried to lift on tiptoe to kiss him.

But his grip tightened. He held her in place. "I can't believe what a blind-ass jerk I am. I was all over Gus for putting moves on you. And all the time, it was me. *I* was the one who wanted to get with you."

Even through the fog of her determined desire, she understood what he was telling her. "Today. When you went into Gus's office with him…"

Jericho nodded. "I went in there to tell him to leave you alone, that you didn't need him chasing after you, that you had been hurt and you needed time to get past that. He set me straight, made me see that he wasn't the one with the problem."

"I'm a problem?" It didn't sound like a good thing.

"No," he said. "You're not a problem. I am."

She took his hand from her shoulder and eased her smaller fingers between his big ones, twining them together into one single fist. "Believe me. This isn't a problem. This is…I don't know. Like a gift I didn't realize I needed."

"Marnie." He looked down at her, so serious. So…concerned. "I'm not a good bet, you know? I'm doing okay in my life now. But I like it on my own. I'm not up for any long-term thing, not into settling down."

"It's not an issue. It's perfect, in fact. All I want from you is right now, tonight."

"Are you sure?"

"Oh, yeah. I'm sure."

He clearly wasn't. "You have to know what this is. It's a classic rebound maneuver. The guy you love hurt you, and you're looking for someone to ease your pain."

How could she argue with that? He was right. "And that's bad?"

"I didn't say it was bad, exactly."

"You can be…my hot rebound guy. Would that work for you?"

"Well, yeah. It would." He added, more enthusiastically, "Hell, yeah." Still, he looked worried. Concerned for her. Foolish man. "But I'm not sure that it's fair to you, you know?"

She drew a slow, careful breath. "But see. That's for me to worry about. I'm the one who decides what's fair for me. And I…I really want this, with you. I trust you and I like you. It's kind of weird, I know, given the way we started out. But it's true. All of a sudden, today, right before you first kissed me, I figured it out…"

"What?"

"That I want you. A lot. And at the same time, I know in my heart that you would never hurt me intentionally."

He squeezed the fingers she had twined with his. "You're right. I wouldn't. But you could end up hurt by my actions now, anyway. It's all up in the air for you at this point. You're coming off a big breakup. It's a rough time for you, not a good time to start having sex with your ex-con brother-in-law."

"Maybe not. And I don't care."

"You say that now."

"Jericho, I mean it. I'm willing to take the risk that I'm going to get hurt all over again. It's worth it to me, to feel really alive, finally, after much too long. Because I see now that I haven't been. I guess I didn't realize how…disconnected from my real self I had become. I'm a brave person, believe it or not. And I've been acting like a coward for years now."

He said her name again, softly. Regretfully.

And yes. She was beginning to accept that it wasn't going to happen with him, to realize that she had to stop pushing him. If he didn't feel right about this, well, she had to respect that.

Still, she had one more point to make. "Please. If you turn me down, make it for your sake. Make it because it's not what *you* want. Don't do it for me. Because what I want, right now, I'm willing to step up and claim. What I want is you, Jericho."

He rubbed the back of his neck with the hand she wasn't holding tight. "I just, well, I think that we shouldn't do anything crazy."

She pulled their clasped hands close, pressing them hard between her breasts. "Oh, but don't you see? Crazy is exactly what I want from you. And not crazy in a Tessa's-mentally-disturbed-sister way. Crazy in a wild way. Crazy in a really good, open, brave way." She almost tried to explain to him that it was beyond confidence-building. To want someone who wanted her back.

But no. That was probably more information than he needed at the moment. She was in this for the heat and the thrill. Pity sex was not going to do it for her.

Maybe a little total shamelessness was in order. She released his hand and she stepped back from him. Holding his burning green gaze, she tugged on the sash of the robe. The half bow collapsed and the sash fell away. And then she eased the robe off her shoulders. It dropped to the floor in a whisper of sound.

All she had underneath was her favorite perfume.

She felt beyond naked, standing there, under his gaze. Exposed in a way she could never remember being before. It terrified her. But at the same time, she felt so free.

So completely herself, so exactly the person she was meant to be. Mark's words came to her, *Where is your spark?*

Maybe it had been a valid question after all. Because, since Mark broke it off with her, she *was* changing. And she was beginning to see that the change was for the better.

Jericho stared at her. He looked at her in a deliciously predatory way. "Marnie." He said her name on a strangled whisper. And then he reached for her.

She melted toward him, lifting her arms, offering her mouth. He took it.

Oh, that man knew how to kiss.

When he lifted his head, he captured her face between his big, rough hands. "Listen to me."

She moaned in frustration. "Oh, no. What now?"

"I didn't bring condoms. I thought, since I was going to tell you what a bad idea this was, that you would agree with me. And we wouldn't need them."

"That's all? That you didn't bring condoms?"

"What do you mean, *all?*"

"I'm on the pill. It's not a problem. Any more reasons why you can't make love with me tonight?"

"The family…"

"This isn't about the family. You know that. This is between you and me."

"I can't help feeling it's asking for trouble."

"Well, you're wrong. It's a good thing, a beautiful thing. Oh, Jericho. Deep inside where you live, in the core of you, you know that it is."

Cradling her face so tenderly, he kissed her lips, her nose, her cheeks, her forehead. "You're a seriously determined woman. You know that, Marnie Jones?"

"Yes, I am," she answered proudly. "Any more reasons you're not letting this happen? Speak now. It's your last chance."

"No," he whispered. "No more reasons…"

"Wrap your arms around me, then. And kiss me like there's nothing else in the whole world tonight. Nothing but you. And me. And this…"

He bent close and kissed her. It was exactly the kiss she had asked for. Deep and wet and endlessly arousing. And then he straightened, taking her with him. Hard arms banded around her, he lifted her feet right off the floor. She wrapped her legs around him and went on kissing him as he started walking.

"Bedroom?" he groaned against her parted lips.

She stuck out a hand and pointed the way.

Chapter Six

Marnie moaned in excited expectation when he laid her down on the bed.

She pulled him down on top of her. And then she reached down between them and touched him, cradling him through his worn-out jeans. He groaned into her mouth and pressed against her hand.

Iron-hard. Burning hot.

His pleasured groan, the way he pushed against her palm…it was all the encouragement she needed. She got to work on his belt buckle, got it undone and open. She fumbled with the metal buttons at his fly, easing them free as fast as she could.

He wasn't wearing anything underneath, a fact that increased her already-considerable arousal. He sprang out, into her waiting hand, hard and thick, smooth as silk, hot as forged iron, a drop of thick moisture weeping from the slit.

She already had her legs around him, her eager hand encircling him. She rubbed that drop of moisture around the head, and loved it when he shuddered, his big body yearning.

Hers to command.

And she couldn't wait. She surged up, guiding him into position....

There. Right there....

She let out another moan, a deeper one, a sound that hovered between a purr and a growl as she felt him nudging her, touching her at exactly the place that she wanted him, yearned for him.

And then, with a hard, quick thrust of his lean hips, he slid into her. She was so wet, so eager, so open for him, she took him fully with that first thrust.

So good. It felt so good, the way he filled her, completely. He groaned in pleasure and went on kissing her, his big hands on either side of her head, his hot fingers tangled in her hair as he began to move.

Oh, that was even better—when he moved. It was exactly what she hungered for, what she hadn't even known she craved. His jeans chaffed the tender skin between her thighs and every stroke seemed to take him even deeper, to push her ever higher.

She reveled in it, gloried in it, in every strong, focused thrust.

She whispered, "Yes, more. Oh! Like that..." Over and over as he moved within her and her body answered him, rocking in time with him.

And then, all at once, so swiftly, she was coming,

rising to the peak and going over, falling endlessly. Soaring.

He surged into her, even deeper than before. She felt him pulsing, giving himself over. She clutched his hips in her two hands, dug her nails in and held on tight, whispering, "Yes. That's it. Right there. Oh, yes…"

In time, he got up and took off all his clothes. He was so beautiful naked. All hard muscle and male power.

He made love to her slowly the second time, pushing her hands away when she tried to urge him to hurry. He laughed, green eyes low and lazy, when she pleaded with him, when she insisted he was driving her crazy— he laughed and then he lowered his head between her thighs once again.

Even though she shoved at his big shoulders, he wouldn't give in and do it her way. Trying to move him when he wasn't going to be moved was like trying to push a boulder up a hill.

In the end, she surrendered to his intimate kiss and was rewarded in the best way possible: with sweet, hot pleasure that built to a finish of shimmering fire.

When the fire resolved into a soft, happy glow, she realized she was starving. They got up and raided the refrigerator and then went back to bed. He turned on his stomach and she settled in close. Across the broadest part of his back, shoulder to shoulder, he had a beautiful tattoo of an eagle, proud wings spread, in a halo of black spikes. She traced the outline of the spikes idly with a finger, on the nape of his powerful neck. And she remembered that first day, in Tessa's living room, when she'd seen those same spikes rising up from under the collar of his T-shirt and been so irrationally afraid.

That seemed impossible now, that she could ever have been scared of this man.

"This is nice," she said drowsily.

He chuckled, snaking out an arm and pulling her in tight. "Nice? I thought you were looking for crazy and wild."

"And I got it. I got exactly what I was looking for." She turned her face to him, kissed him long and lingeringly and then whispered against his mouth, "But right now, this is nice. Very, very nice."

They napped for little while. And then they made love again.

Later, they talked about the chopper he was making for Ash's charity event, the Texas State Endowment Ball. The family company, BravoCorp, was sponsoring the ball this year. The proceeds from the auction were going to provide financial aid and various goods and services for needy families all over Texas. The ball and auction was happening May 1, a Saturday, just two and a half weeks away.

He smoothed her tangled hair back from her forehead. "Got your fancy dress yet?"

"I didn't know I was going."

"You're going," he said, which really was news to her.

"And you know this how?"

"The family is going and you're part of the family. Plus, I want you there. And I'll still be your boss then, so you have to do what I say."

"Pushy, pushy—and I thought Gus was my boss."

"He's your supervisor. We're both your boss."

"It's not easy being an underling."

"Save the date. You *are* going."

"Okay, okay." She had two long dresses hanging in the closet that might work. But she'd bought both of them with Mark's money. Uh-uh. For this, she wanted something new, something with no memories attached. Which meant she would have to buy one and it would cost her more than she really ought to spend. Maybe Tessa could point her toward a good consignment shop.

"You're too quiet," he said. "All right. If you don't want to go—"

"Shh." She put her fingers to his soft lips. "I have my orders and I plan to obey them."

He grunted. "Frankly, I don't see obedience as a long suit with you."

"Maybe not. But I'm making an exception in this case."

"Because I'm your boss."

"And because, the more I think it over, the more I want to go. I want to see that bike you're building bring six figures."

"Yeah. I wish."

"Hey. It could happen."

"Anything's possible, I guess." He reached across her to turn the nightstand clock so he could see it. "Almost midnight." And then he kissed her.

They made love one more time and he left at a little after one.

In the morning, when she woke, she turned to the empty side of the bed and then braced up on an elbow to run her hand across the stretch of wrinkled sheet where he had been. She pressed her nose into his pillow and smelled the scent of his skin on the soft cotton of the pillowcase.

And then she yawned and stretched, feeling the soreness in her most tender places, a good kind of ache. She felt well used, acutely female in a way she couldn't remember feeling before.

It had been a good night. The best. She shut her eyes and relived a few of the highlights all over again, sighing a little, her heart beating faster, just at the memory.

But later, as she showered, dressed for work and ate a quick breakfast, the events of the night just past kind of took on a hazy, dreamlike quality. And really, it was definitely weird, that she would go to work and come face-to-face with her boss, who was also her brother-in-law, after seeing him naked the night before.

She started kind of second-guessing herself, losing the joy of what had happened, thinking about how aggressive she'd been, how she'd practically demanded that he have sex with her. At the time, it had all seemed so hot and inevitable.

Now, well, if she let herself, she could feel a little foolish.

Scratch that. A *lot* foolish.

Tessa showed up from the other house just as she was leaving. "Is everything all right?" she asked when Marnie opened the door.

"Sure. Why?"

"Is something going on with you and Jericho?"

"Why?"

"One of those custom cars from his shop was parked in the driveway half the night."

"Is that a problem?"

Tessa gave her a long look. "Well, I don't know. Is it?" She was wearing her Saint Teresa expression, all pinched up and tight. Clearly, Tessa did not approve of Marnie having wild sex with their brother-in-law.

Marnie stepped back. "Come on in. I've got maybe fifteen minutes and then I really have to get to work."

Tessa sat on the couch. "So, you and Jericho?" She wrapped her arms around herself. "You're having…a thing?"

Marnie sat beside her. "What we're having is a totally torrid love affair. Why? Is that not okay with you?"

Tessa gulped. "It's only, well, do you think that's wise?"

"Truthfully, Tessa, I don't know about wise. Maybe not. I do think it's…really good. And I could use something really good in my life about now."

"Really good, how?"

Marnie raked her fingers back through her hair. "Come on. Stop with the endless questions. If you have something to say, just say it."

Tessa made a low, pained sound. "I don't think he's looking for a permanent relationship, that's all."

"I know he's not. But it's fine. Neither of us is."

Tessa looked like she was getting a headache. "I don't understand this. You just got your heart broken. Why ask for trouble all over again?"

Marnie turned, took both her sister's hands. "Tessa. Seriously. I don't believe I'm asking for trouble at all."

"I think you're misguided."

"What can I say? Sometimes, you know, it's about the journey."

Tessa made a scoffing sound. "The journey."

Marnie felt defensive. Definitely defensive. And shallow, somehow. And like something of a mental case, which she knew both Tessa and Ash worried that she was.

Still, she tried to keep her tone even and reasonable. "Yeah. That's right. The journey. I really like him, a lot. And I'm *really* attracted to him."

"But you hardly know him. And you've only just broken up with Mark, after all these years."

"So? I've got to live like a nun, just me and my poor broken heart?"

"I didn't say that. I don't like it, that's all. I think that Jericho's taking advantage of you."

That was a good one. "You think *he's* taking advantage of *me?* Wrong. He really tried to turn me down. But I kept begging."

"You're exaggerating."

"Well, okay. Maybe a little. I didn't beg. I was just relentlessly reasonable. Until he finally gave in." She remembered the way she'd dropped the robe from her shoulders and stood there in front of him, wearing nothing but a hopeful smile. She softened her tone. "Tessa, I know you're only sticking your nose where it shouldn't be because you love me."

"And I'm *worried* about you."

"I know. But, well, think of your own life, all the chances you took with the wrong guys. And things have worked out pretty well for you."

"It's not the same."

Marnie couldn't let that stand. "Remember Bill?" Okay, it was something of a low blow. Bill Toomey had been Tessa's last boyfriend before Ash. Tessa had been planning to marry Bill. The day she got the letter from him saying it was over, she met Ash—during a blizzard. They were snowed in together for a couple of days. And they'd wasted no time getting to know each other.

Intimately.

Tessa pulled her hands free and repeated, "It's not the same."

Marnie had sense enough to be silent. She watched her sister's face as Tessa remembered. And slowly came to understand.

Tessa shook her head. "Now you're telling me that Jericho is the guy for you?"

"I'm telling you that not every love affair ends in happily ever after. But if you don't take a few chances, well, you can end up staying with the wrong guy—or missing the moment with the *right* one."

"I guess I just want to protect you. I don't want you to be hurt ever again."

"Too bad. Hurting's part of being alive. Even my favorite big sister can't protect me from that."

Tessa stared at her. "You are becoming fearless, I think. Just like when you were a kid. And yeah, that does scare me, at least a little."

"It scares me some, too. But I'm not letting that hold me back. Not ever again."

Softly, Tessa asked, "And Mark? You're really over him, then?"

If a girl can't tell the truth to her sister, well, who can she say it to? "Uh-uh. No. I'm not over Mark, not really."

"So, if he came to you, here in Texas, if he wanted you to go back to him…?"

"I don't know. I like to tell myself I wouldn't go, not if he crawled through broken glass, pleading for another chance, bleeding all over himself…" She let the words trail off.

Tessa prompted, "But?"

Marnie confessed, "I might be tempted, if he came after me. I loved him so much—still do. We have serious history together, Mark and me. Remember that year he and I were ten, when he ran away from his dad?"

"I remember," said her sister disapprovingly. "The whole town was in an uproar, looking for him. And you wouldn't tell Uncle Jack where he was." Their uncle had been a sheriff's deputy back then.

"I knew it was wrong, what Mark did, running away, scaring everyone. He stayed away for days, remember?"

"I'll never forget."

"And I knew *I* was wrong, to help him. It wasn't like all the times I ran away. I always either got found in the first few hours, or came home on my own the same day I left. But not Mark. He was in it for the long haul. He was going to get his dad to deal with him and the issues they had, or he wasn't coming back. So I told him where to hide, sneaked food out of the house to take to him. Because he was my *friend,* you know? My true friend. We were…I don't know, bonded, I guess you could say. From that first winter he came to town onward. We were blood brothers. Seriously. We actually sliced our palms with a pocket knife and pressed them together, swearing undying loyalty to each other."

Tessa was not impressed. "Euu. When was that?"

"The year Mark and I were both nine, the winter of that first year you and I came back from Arkansas to live with Dad and Gina." Marnie let out a sad little chuckle. "Mark fainted at the sight of all that blood. I held his bloody hand in mine until he came to."

"God. That's just scary, you know?"

"Yeah. Maybe. I still feel it, though, the bond with him. And I'm past the burning fury stage now when I think of him. I can kind of see why he ended it." She tapped the side of her head. "I know in here now that it wasn't right with us, that we weren't a good match. He's grown up to be a nice, solid, stable guy. And I'm…well, I'm just not. To be happy and complete, I need a little edge in my life. I couldn't care less about sound investments or money in the bank, or living in the 'right' neighborhood and knowing the right people."

Tessa whispered sadly, "But those things really do matter to Mark."

"Yes, they do. It just wasn't working with us. My brain has gotten that message." She laid her hand above her heart. "But in here, I'm kind of slow to learn my lesson. In here, I wonder how he's doing, if he's happy, if maybe he still thinks of me and wishes that it had gone differently."

"Marnie, listen to yourself. You're saying you still love him."

"Uh-uh. I'm saying that I'm not totally over him. But I am working on it. And every day I feel a little more sure of who *I* am and what I need to make a life that works for me."

"But you *would* go back to him if he—"

Marnie held up a hand. "It's not going to happen. And I am moving on."

Tessa straightened the collar of the white shirt she was wearing.

The fussy movement tipped Marnie off. "What else? You're fidgeting."

"Well, I asked Ash to have a word with Jericho, to try to get him to leave you alone."

Marnie groaned. "You're getting to be as bad as Grandpa, you know that? So sure of how other people ought to run their lives."

Tessa busted to it. "You're right. I went too far. In my own defense, though, it was only out of love."

"Yeah, well, call off the dogs."

Marnie made it to work on time, barely.

Gus was behind the counter when she walked in. But he usually came in before seven, like Jericho. Both of them were pretty much married to SA Choppers.

He asked with a gleam in those dark eyes, "Seen Rico?"

Her ears felt suddenly warm. She really hoped she wasn't blushing. "He's not here?"

"Big Jake said he was, but then he got a call and left."

A call. From Ash? Her heart kind of stuttered to a stop for a second before it started beating again. "A call from…?"

"If I knew, would I be asking you?"

"Guess not. And sorry, I don't know where he's gone." And really, that call could have been from anyone. Plus, Tessa had promised she'd tell Ash to back off. If Ash had called his brother before Tessa reached him, well, for sure she must have gotten a hold of him by now.

Gus said, "You're on the counter."

"Got it."

He turned and went through the door at the back, into the main shop, the dogs trailing in his wake. Marnie dug her cell out of her purse and autodialed her sister.

"Did you talk to Ash?"

"His cell went straight to voicemail. I left him a message there and also at the office," Tessa said. "But he hasn't called me back yet."

"I'm at work. Gus says Jericho got a call and left suddenly."

"That doesn't mean he's meeting Ash. And it's not the end of the world, anyway, I'm sure."

"Yeah. Well, as soon as you talk to him and tell him to leave his poor brother alone, call me."

"I will, I promise."

Jericho slid into the coffee-shop booth opposite Ash. He flipped his cup over and the waitress filled it. When she left, he turned to his brother, who was watching him, wearing a grim expression that did nothing to put Jericho at ease.

"Okay. I'm here. What?"

Ash stirred his coffee, though he always took it black. "Tessa asked me to talk to you." Just the tone of his voice told Jericho way more than he wanted to know. Ash leveled an accusing look at him. "One of your cars was in the driveway all night."

Jericho said nothing. What was there to say?

Ash spoke again. "You spent the night in the guesthouse."

Jericho sipped his coffee. "Most of it. Yeah."

"Why would you do that?"

"Do what?"

"You're being purposely dense. You know what. Take advantage of Marnie like that?"

Jericho almost laughed at that one. His brother didn't know Marnie very well. "She's a great woman." He said the words flatly. "I like her. A lot."

"She's in a…weakened state right now. You said it yourself that first night you met her."

"I said I thought she was on drugs, or in need of a shrink. I was wrong. Dead wrong."

"I'll ask you again. Why would do that?"

He thought about Marnie. She was not only a great woman, she was a determined one. He had a lot of respect for her, more than ever after last night. And a yen. A big one. Just thinking about her, remembering her dropping that skimpy little robe off her shoulders, had him getting hard. And not only the way she looked naked. So much more. The sweet, clean scent of her skin, the sound of her eager moans when he was inside her…

Gus had been right. She did it for him. In a big way.

Ash said, "You know she doesn't need to get into it with you right now, Rico. What in God's name were you thinking?"

"You know, Ash. I don't see that it's any of your business."

"She's my wife's sister. My wife's sister who needs us to help her, not mess her over even worse than she already is."

Jericho felt his temper flare. In his family, he'd always been the loser, the screwup, the one who never failed to wreck a good thing. Ash, on the other hand, was everything Jericho wasn't. Smooth and smart. A born CEO. The one who did everything right.

Mostly, Jericho thought of himself as over that old crap—the seething resentment, the jealousy. But right now, sitting across from his perfect oldest brother, getting lectured on how he'd screwed up again, well, it brought a bitter taste to his mouth, resurrected the old pain of not being good enough, not *Bravo* enough. And that made the skin on the back of his neck feel tight and his blood race hot and angry through his veins.

He spoke more softly. "A couple of points."

"What?"

"One, I think you're seriously underestimating Marnie. And two, she's herself, first of all. Before she's anybody's sister. What happened with us last night is between her and me. Period."

Ash leaned across the table and opened his mouth to continue the lecture. Jericho tried not to think about how satisfying it would be to punch his perfect brother in the face.

But then Ash's cell rang. He sat back, pulled an iPhone out of his inside pocket, looked at the display, then put it to his ear. "I'm with Jericho right now," he said. And then, kind of startled, "What?" And next,

"But I thought you said…" Jericho could hear the feminine voice on the other end of the line. He knew it was Tessa. When she stopped talking, Ash said gently, "You know, you kind of put me in a position here…" Tessa started in again. Ash started nodding. "All right. Yeah. Okay…I will…Okay." He disconnected the call and tucked the phone away.

Jericho said, "So I'm guessing that Tessa talked with Marnie."

Ash turned the handle of his coffee cup from left to right. "I still don't think what you did was right."

"But it's none of your business, big brother, now, is it?"

Ash met his eyes. "You're right. It's none of my business."

The thing was, Jericho agreed with the harsh stuff Ash had laid on him.

To a degree, anyway. Even with all the yadda-yadda he and Marnie had gone through last night before she finally convinced him to quit telling her what was good for her and just take what he wanted, he still felt kind of bad. Kind of like he had done what Ash had accused him of, used her, moved in on her when she was vulnerable and easily manipulated.

Bottom line, Marnie *didn't* need another man in her life now. And even though Ash had admitted he had no right to stick his face in it, the things he'd said were still there, still ugly, scrolling through Jericho's brain.

He was starting to see that maybe last night had been a big, beautiful, super-hot mistake. That maybe going on with it would only make things worse.

At the shop, he saw her dusty little black car in front. He took the coward's way out and went in through the back, racing straight up the steel stairway to his private workshop and getting right to work.

An hour later, he was dealing with some issues he had with the gas tank on the chopper for Ash's charity ball. It was a special design, sort of an extended peanut, long and narrow, curving down sharply toward the seat, and he'd yet to figure out how to attach it without gaps. The whole point, after all, was the sleek, mean appearance. It had to look all of one bad, killer piece.

He'd already modified one of the three basic chassis he used, all his own designs. But it was looking like further modification was in order. That was going to slow down the work by a day or two and that had him going back to the tank design itself, seeing if he could make the changes on it before fabrication.

He'd tuned out everything but the job by then. So he didn't hear Marnie come up the stairs. By the time he happened to glance in her direction, she could have been standing there for half an hour, for all he knew.

His heart gave a jump and then one single, hard beat, like a fist bump, against the wall of his chest, as he straightened from the drafting table. "Hey."

"Hey." She was standing at the top of the stairs. But when she spoke, she started toward him. She wore her usual work clothes—tight jeans, sneakers, an SA Choppers T-shirt and a hat with the shop logo on it. Except for the tightness of the jeans, there was nothing all that exciting about the way she dressed.

But he *was* excited. Just from watching her come

toward him. His own jeans kept getting tighter, the closer she got.

This was bad, he knew it. Bad and getting worse.

He never should have started with her. It wasn't good for her—and it was too damn distracting for him. He was plain ridiculous over her, already, unable to watch her walk toward him without getting turned on.

She stopped a few feet from him and looked down at the drawing table. "Gus said you were an artist. You are."

He rubbed the back of his neck. It still felt strange and naked, without his long hair. "You come up here to talk about choppers?"

She swiped off the hat and her shoulder-length hair came loose. It was straight. Brown with pale streaks. The feel of it, he had learned last night, was so smooth and fine. His hands itched to touch it.

And then she moved closer.

Chapter Seven

When she stopped, there was maybe a foot's distance between them.

He could smell her. Rain. She kind of smelled like rain.

Who knew that the smell of rain would make him think of sex?

"No," she said. "Not about choppers."

It took him a second or two to remember that he'd asked her if she came up here to talk about bikes. "I didn't think so." He let his hand drop to his side and fisted it, to keep from reaching out and reeling her in.

Not reaching didn't do him any good. *She* reached out—or rather, up. She slid her hand over his T-shirt, fingers curving, feeling his flesh beneath. He had to steel himself to keep from yowling like a tomcat on the scent of a female in heat, just at her touch.

She brushed the backs of her fingers along his throat, making his Adam's apple burn until he had to swallow—and then she reached back and clasped the nape of his neck.

It was the moment to tell her they had to cut this crap out. But he didn't say a damn thing, just gathered her against him when she went on tiptoe, offering her mouth.

She kissed him. He kissed her back. The blood was thick and slow in his veins.

And his pants were tighter by the second.

She moved even closer, rubbed herself against him. She knew exactly what she was doing.

He thought of the daybed over in the corner, of dragging her over there and unzipping her jeans. It was a minor miracle he stayed where he was. And it was beyond unbelievable that he somehow managed to take her by the waist and lift his mouth from the hot, wet, seduction of hers.

"Don't even think it," she whispered.

He crooked an eyebrow and tried to look like he had everything under control.

Eventually, after gazing up at him for several heat-charged seconds, her expression both dreamy and smug, she said, "You don't want to end this. Not yet. You know you don't."

"Now you're a mind reader."

She gave him a slow smile. "Well, it's not exactly your mind I'm reading here."

"It's hard being a guy. Literally."

They both laughed at his bad joke, which kind of eased the tension a little. Then she took his hand and led him over to the daybed and pulled him down next to her.

"Anybody could come up those stairs," he reminded her. From below in the shop, rising up from under the sound of heavy metal music, came the scream of a saw cutting steel.

She sighed. "I know. And I didn't drag you over here to get you to have sex with me."

"No?"

"No—even though I think that we really should come up here one of these nights when no one else is in the shop. Because I could definitely do you in your place of work."

"Is sex all you think about?"

She butted her shoulder against him. "Well, yeah. Since yesterday. When you kissed me. It's like some old fifties song. You kissed me. Ka-pow. That did it. Doo-wop, doo-wop, sh-boom, baby—and I know you had coffee with Ash this morning."

He slumped back into the sagging cushions and stared in the general direction of the punching bag and free weights over in the corner, where he took out his frustrations when a project wasn't going right. He wished he was working the bag about now.

Marnie said, "I take it from your expression that it didn't go well with Ash."

He grunted. "Tessa called him to tell him never mind, but he was already in the middle of reaming me a new one by then."

"She told me. And she's sorry she butted in. And Ash is sorry, too. Everybody's sorry. We need to just get over it and move on."

"Marnie, *you* need to think about where this is going—which is pretty much nowhere."

"Uh-uh. You're wrong. You listened to whatever crap Ash was feeding you. It's not his business. You should have told him that."

"I did. It had no effect on him. Until Tessa called. Then he backed off."

"You noticed your big brother is a little bit whipped?"

"Yeah, so? He's happy. Really happy."

"And good for him. Good for both of them. But they're not us. We need to remember that."

"*You* need to remember, Marnie. There is no us."

She made a hissing sound, tongue curved just behind her neat white teeth. "Don't be cruel. There *is* an us. At the moment, anyway." Suddenly she was all cheerful briskness. "And I've been thinking."

"Now I'm *really* scared."

"Two things I want from you—I mean, beyond the basic hotness thing."

He knew he shouldn't ask. "What two things?"

"First, I want you to teach me to ride a chopper."

He laughed. "Wasn't once enough?"

"No." She was looking way too serious.

He tried to make her see what a dangerous idea that was. "Most choppers just aren't designed to fit a woman. You'll be on your toes when you put your feet down and you have to slide forward in the seat to reach the brake pedal."

"Yeah, so? I know that."

"It's all fine as long as there are no surprises. But you're looking for disaster at your first unplanned stop."

"Little Ted is shorter than me." Little Ted was one of his builders. "I'll bet he's built something to fit him."

"You just don't go taking a man's ride." Although she had done exactly that the day they met. She remembered, too. She grinned. He rolled his eyes.

And she went right back to working on him. "Most of the guys around here have more than one. One to spare, even. And I could pay like rent—well, at least a little."

"Marnie…"

She just looked at him. Determined. And hopeful. How did she do that? With a look, she could convince him of just about any harebrained thing.

He shut his eyes, shook his head. "Give me a couple of days. Let me see if I can come up with something safe for you to ride."

She let out a whoop and jumped up, hitching a leg over him, straddling him. "You are so completely my hero!" She bent close and kissed him, making a loud, smacking sound.

He snorted. "Save the gratitude for after I get you a ride—*if* I manage it."

She planted another smacker on him. "You will. I know you will."

He caught her by the waist—and liked the feel of her between his hands. Liked it way too much. He looked up into her shining baby-blue eyes. "That all? I have to work, you know."

"So do I. The other thing?"

"Yeah. What?"

"I've never seen where you live. Do you have an apartment? Your own house?"

"I've got a house. It's not very big. In a so-so neighborhood. It calls out for a close encounter with a few cans of fresh paint."

"Great. Can I come over?"

"Why?"

"I want to see it."

"Seriously? There's not much to see."

"Doesn't matter. I like you. I want to know more about you—like, you know, where you live."

"I'll think about it."

She hitched her leg back across him and plopped down beside him again. "What's the big deal?"

"Marnie. Let me take care of getting you a chopper that you're not going to kill yourself on. Then we'll talk about you coming to my place."

She pulled a long face. "And I thought getting you to teach me to ride was going to be the hard one."

"It's only that it's not real comfortable. I barely go there myself, except to shower, change clothes and sleep. Don't make a big deal out of it, okay?"

"All right." She grabbed his hand, stood and towed him up with her, quickly sliding her arms under his and pulling him close. "You will be relieved to know that I'm going back to work now. One kiss and I'm out of here."

"Promises, promises…"

"Tonight. The guesthouse. About eight, like last night?"

He gave in without argument. Why draw it out? She'd only convince him to come to her in the end. "Okay. Eight."

"I like it when you say yes." She had her head tipped back as she looked up at him.

Her lips were too tempting. He bent and kissed her. She tasted so good, like nobody else, and the scent of her teased him.

When he let her go, she scooped her hat up off the corner of his drawing table and bounced away down the stairs.

That night, Ash and Tessa went out to dinner, which was great with Marnie. She grabbed a sandwich and then she took a long bath. By seven-thirty she was bathed and scented and waiting impatiently for Jericho, wearing nothing but the itty-bitty robe she'd worn the night before.

Her cell rang at quarter to eight. Her heart sank at the sound. She just knew it would be Jericho, getting a serious case of scruples again, calling to tell her he'd changed his mind about seeing her anymore.

But then she looked at the display. *Grandpa Oggie.* At least it wasn't Jericho bowing out. But still…

Just what she needed. Her nosy grandpa telling her what to do.

She made a face at the phone and considered not answering. But in the end, she knew he wouldn't give up until he'd reached her and worn her ear off with platitudes and unwanted advice. And besides, a phone call was better than his showing up in the flesh.

"Hi, Grandpa. How you doing?"

"Marnie?" he shouted. For as long as she could remember, he always shouted when he talked on the phone. "That you?"

She winced. Who else would it be? She turned the sound down about halfway. "Yes, Grandpa. It's me. How are you?"

"Speak up. Can't hear you."

She shouted back at him. "How are you?"

"Me? I'm old, that about says it all. And that ain't the question anyway. I called to find out how *you* are."

"I'm doing fine, really. No need to worry over me."

"How long you been out there at Tessa's?"

She figured it was a trick question, just from his tone. But she answered, anyway. "Two weeks. As of today."

"Two damn weeks." He mumbled something under his breath and then started yelling again. "Nobody tells me squat around here, you know that? I heard you and Mark Drury were quits from Linda Lou Beardsly just today. That hurt my pride, girl, to think that old battle-ax knew more about my own granddaughter than I did." Linda Lou was almost as old as her grandpa, an upright church lady who knew everything that went on in town. "I went straight to Gina," he said. "She confessed it was true."

"I asked them not to tell you. I...didn't want to worry you."

Her grandpa let out one of his cackling rumbles of laughter. "You didn't want me to drive out there and look after you. That's what you didn't want."

"Well, I—"

"Don't give me no lies, girl. I'm too old to wade through a big pile of bull crap. And you don't have to worry about me showin' up there. Not in the near future, anyway. I'm not getting around so good."

"What are you saying? Are you sick?" Her grandpa *never* got sick. Even though he was past ninety, she simply could not picture him ever becoming a truly old person—someone who needed other people to care for him. Someone fading away toward the end.

"Hell, no, I ain't sick. I never get sick." At his words, a warm feeling of relief had her letting out the breath she hadn't realized she was holding. He added, "My foot's been botherin' me somethin' fierce lately, though." He'd shot it half off years ago, supposedly while cleaning his rifle, although some claimed he did it on purpose—why, exactly, Marnie never knew. "And my old bones ache. That's the worst thing about bein' a relic. A man can't come to the aid of his blood kin when they need him. There was a time I'd already be behind the wheel, on my way to you."

She shouted with great firmness, "Grandpa. I mean it. Do not come to Texas. I am doing great, really."

"Well, I can't say as I'm surprised to hear that."

"Uh. You're not?"

"Hell, no. That Mark Drury's a nice boy. But he never was the one for you."

"Gee, Grandpa. *Now* you tell me."

"Well, I hate to butt in with my opinions when nobody's listenin'."

"Hah."

"What was that? Speak up."

"I said, oh yes. I know that."

He cackled some more. "You always were the feisty one. Remember that time you stole my Cadillac? You were what, eleven or so? And you always were a scrawny, short little thing. Your feet could barely reach the gas pedal. But you didn't let that stop you. You're lucky you didn't run off the highway into the river and break your fool neck."

"Yes, Grandpa," she answered wearily. "I remember." Jericho's bike. Her grandpa's El Dorado. She really had to stop stealing people's vehicles.

"And that time you stole that big fishbowl of jawbreakers from Santino's store? You poured them all in a rubber boot and tossed the boot up in a tree, as I recall. Gina had to take you down to the sheriff's station, where they gave you a lecture to try to scare some sense into you. I don't believe it did a bit of good."

Marnie said nothing. She figured he'd only take any comment she made as encouragement to continue re-minding her of all the crazy-ass stuff she'd done as a kid.

More cackling from her grandfather's end. "You were just trouble waiting to happen."

"Thanks," she said sourly.

"Until you got to be twelve or thirteen, that is. You seemed to get some control of yourself by then. And frankly, the past few years, since you been with the Drury boy, it's like a light went out in you. I'm glad to hear you kicked over the traces and reclaimed your own real self."

Like she had a choice. But she had to admit that his praise was rather gratifying. "I'm working on it, Grandpa," she shouted modestly.

"I want you to call me, anytime. You need to talk, you pick up the phone."

Really, he was being kind of sweet. In spite of the endless reminders of her checkered past. "Thanks, Grandpa. I will." She wouldn't, but he didn't need to know that.

His rheumy chuckle rolled out. "You're lyin'. But it's okay. Never hurts to be nice to your old grandpa. You need money?"

"Everyone asks me that."

"It's 'cause we care."

"Yeah. I know. And no, thank you, I'm getting by just fine."

"Well, all right, then. I'll be in touch."

The line went quiet. She hit the off button and set the phone down, glancing up fast when she heard the light tap on the glass door.

Jericho.

She jumped up and ran to let him in, grabbing him in a hug, tipping her head back to grin up at him. "You smell like soap and gasoline. And leather, too. It's very sexy."

He laid his hand on the side of her face. "And you just plain smell good." He kissed her, a tender, quick kiss. When she pulled away to close the blinds and the curtains, he said, "I watched you for a minute or two, talking on the phone. You looked happy."

"I was talking to my grandpa. He's a crazy old guy who sticks his nose in everybody's business. But, well, we all know it's because he cares."

"You were shouting."

"Yeah. He's hard of hearing—at least on the phone. He just wanted to know that I was doing okay. *And* to remind me of my various exploits as a kid." She stepped up close to him again. She liked being close, liked the feel of his body heat, the look in his eyes. A hungry look. Hungry for her…

He ran the rough pad of his index finger along the slight inner swell of her left breast, down into the deep V where her robe overlapped in the center of her chest—and then back up again, tracing the curve. The light touch sent a burning shiver through her, made her sigh in anticipation.

She pulled the sash end and the robe fell open. He slid it off her shoulders.

"You are something special," he whispered, bending closer, nuzzling the sensitive skin near her ear. She tipped her head to give him better access and moaned low when his teeth closed over her earlobe. He bit down gently at first and then slowly increased the pressure. It didn't hurt, exactly. But almost. He took the small, sharp, contained pressure right to the edge of pain and then he used his tongue to stroke the tender flesh that his teeth held captive.

Moisture flooded between her legs. Her knees went wobbly.

Not that the wobbliness mattered. She didn't need to hold herself upright because he scooped her off her feet and carried her into the other room.

Jericho loved the way she wrapped herself around him. Until now, he'd always preferred tall, shapely women, big women with full hips and large breasts.

Marnie wasn't tall. She had slim hips and small, pretty breasts with perfect, delicate pink nipples. Not his type.

Until now.

Now, he was learning, there was a serious upside for a tall man with a smaller woman. She was easy to lift, all angles and tight flesh. There was a certain toughness to her, an inner steel, that made him feel he could do what he wanted with her, that it was safe to lose himself in the taste and feel of her, in the clean smell of her skin.

Before her, small women kind of scared him. He was afraid of hurting them, of crushing them beneath his much greater size and weight.

But not Marnie. She could take it. She was strong—and also slim and smooth. She felt so good, so right, so fearless—her legs clasping his waist, her arms twined around his neck, her straight brown hair brushing his shoulder as she tipped her head to capture his mouth, her quick, hot little tongue sliding between his lips, rubbing the edges of his teeth, teasing his own tongue, twining with it.

She had herself so tightly wound around him, he could slide his hands along the velvet skin at the backs of her thighs without worrying he might drop her. He could cup her hard little bottom, dip his fingers into the slick, wet curls that covered her sex. She moaned into his mouth and speared her tongue in deeper as he stroked her, easing his fingers along the silky secret flesh, opening her, going hard as a flag pole at the wet, eager feel of her.

Beside the bed, he slid his hands back under her thighs. She instantly picked up his cue and unhooked her ankles from around his waist. He guided her down so her feet touched the floor. She lowered her arms from around his neck, dragging her fingernails down his chest, one hard, long caress, to his belt buckle, which she went right to work on. He helped her, pulling his shirt off and throwing it behind him while she undid the buckle and then ripped his fly wide.

She sank to her knees in front of him, her head tipped back, eyelids low and lazy. He looked down, into those eyes that challenged him and wanted him and also seemed to admire him, which kind of scared him a little.

But not enough to insist they had to call it off. Truthfully, he didn't know what it would take to get him to call it off with her.

A lot. Which was why he was here with her, drowning in her blue eyes, quivering beneath the soft, knowing touch of her slim hands as she pushed his pants down around his ankles and then cupped his shins, her touch gliding back up, over his knees. Higher.

She would be gone within a few too-short weeks, he kept reminding himself. Why not enjoy her while he had the chance? She wanted it. And he wanted it. What harm could it do?

Okay, a lot. He had to admit that. She could get hurt. He could get hurt. Already, because he couldn't keep his hands off her, there was renewed tension between him and Ash.

Ash didn't get it—why he'd want to get into it with Tessa's sister like this. Ash knew that Jericho was not about to make it permanent with any woman. And Ash still saw Marnie as a little unbalanced, as someone in need of support and extra care.

Jericho didn't see her as weak or unbalanced. Not anymore. He knew now that she was tougher than she even realized.

She captured him in her right hand, wrapping her fingers around him, squeezing, but carefully. It felt so good. He closed his eyes and let a groan of pure pleasure escape him.

And then her mouth was there, wet and hot, surrounding him, taking him in, deep, so he slid right past the back wall of her throat—and then letting him out again. She repeated the deep stroke. Again.

And again.

He let her take him right to the edge, moving in time with her, flexing his hips backward and then forward, into her eager heat. When he felt the end coming, he reached down, captured her face between his hands, and made a low, protesting sound to get her to stop before he lost it completely.

She pretended not to understand. Or maybe, she was just lost enough, just carried away enough, that she really didn't know what he was trying to tell her. She took him in and let him out, over and over.

"Marnie, you have to…" Words failed him. He groaned low. "Marnie. Stop. You have to stop before I…"

But she didn't stop. And finally, he gave up trying to make her. He gave up everything. He let her soft hands and eager mouth take him over the edge, turn him inside out. Pleasure was a pulse, insistent, overwhelming, beating through him, carrying him to the far reaches of paradise.

He clutched her silky head and poured himself into her. She took him. All of him. Every drop.

Chapter Eight

When his head stopped spinning and the world came into focus again, he looked down at her flushed face, her full, wet mouth. "I tried to…let you know I was about to lose it." His voice sounded strange to his own ears, a rough husk of torn sound.

"I knew it." She smiled, her wet, swollen lips tipping up at the corners. "But I didn't want to stop." She swept upward, onto to her feet. And then she took him by the hand and pulled him down onto the bed with her.

His jeans were tangled at his ankles and he still had his boots on. At that moment, he didn't even care that he probably looked damn ridiculous, all tied up in his own pants. He shut his eyes with a low groan and put his arm across them.

The bed shifted. She slid to the floor again, pulled off his boots, his socks and his jeans.

A moment later, she came back to him. Her soft skin was warm against his side, the scent of her sweet and also musky now. It had turned her on, what she did to him. He could almost get hard again, just from smelling the evidence of her desire. She rested her chin on his chest and he lowered his arm and stroked her hair.

She lifted up enough to press a kiss to his left nipple. And then, with a sigh, she turned over to her back and laid her head on his belly. "You make a great pillow."

"Glad I'm good for something."

"Oh, I do believe you're good for a lot of things."

He traced her eyebrows, one and then the other. "Give me a few minutes. We'll get into the other things I'm good for."

She was moving again, sliding off him, stretching out beside him, bracing on an elbow, resting her free hand on his chest. And then brushing it lower.

He knew where her touch was headed—and it wasn't anywhere sexy. Her fingers found the white ridge of scar tissue on his belly, to the right of his navel.

"What's this?" With the tip of her finger, she followed the long, white shape of the scar, but her gaze was locked with his.

He wasn't planning to answer that. He was going to take her hand and kiss her fingertips and tell her it was nothing.

But then, why do that? Why lie? They didn't have forever together. But at least they could have something honest while it lasted.

"In prison. From a knife made out of a bed slat. Makes a pretty crude cut."

She didn't say anything, which he really appreciated. She just watched his face with those big blue eyes of hers.

He said, "I avoided affiliations inside. It's a quick way to get yourself killed, not having anyone taking your back." He tucked her hair behind her ear, one side and then the other. "There were power plays against me. No one likes a loner. I almost died from that one there on my belly. But I got through it. Sometimes, when I look back, I'm not really sure how."

She leaned closer, sliding across him, until she could press her lips to the scar. His gut tightened. He reached down and put his hand on the back of her head, fingers gliding under the warm strands of her hair.

When she pulled away that time, she turned over on her back a second time, and used his stomach for a pillow again. He studied her profile. She had her eyes closed. She wasn't smiling or frowning. She was just lying there, one hand on the inward curve of her bare stomach, knees drawn up. Quiet. Still.

He smoothed her hair, combing it, finding pleasure in the feel of the strands between his fingers. "When I went in," he said, "I told the family to stay away. My mom came a couple times. And Ash. And Caleb—he's fourth-born. And Gabe, the family lawyer. I wouldn't see them. Eventually, they stopped coming. Not Gus, though. Yeah, I had told him to stay away, too. I'd said if he'd just keep my chopper for me, the only one I had then, the first bike I ever built, that would be all I wanted from him."

She sighed, reached back a hand and brushed the

side of his face, so lightly. But she didn't say a word, didn't open her eyes.

He appreciated that. That she just listened, that she didn't feel she had to pressure him with questions or act all sympathetic at hearing about his shady past. He said, "Gus came anyway, to see me. Once a week, without fail, for two damn years. Even though I refused, every time, to take his visits. Gus can be one determined son of a gun, you know?"

Now she was smiling, a bare hint of a smile. She made a low sound in her throat. Of understanding, maybe? Or satisfaction.

He ran a finger down the center of her forehead, over the clean line of her nose. To her mouth. He touched her lips. So soft. Plump. The rest of her was firm and lean. But those lips…

She stuck out the tip of her tongue, but only enough to brush the pad of his finger with it. He moved that finger onward, over her strong chin, down the tight slope of her throat. Her clavicle was sharply defined. He touched the cage of bone, so hard, sharp beneath the satin of her skin.

He went on, "Finally I got so mad at Gus for not giving up, I agreed to see him. Just once. To tell him what an ass he was being, wasting his time when I didn't want to talk to him. I didn't want to talk to anyone. I was so caught up in my own big drama, in my tough-ass nobility. I was going to go it alone and no one was going to try and help me get through it."

He touched her nipple. She sucked in a small gasp. And then he put his hand over her breast, cupping it, so that pretty little nipple pressed squarely into the center of his palm. His hand looked big and rough against her torso. Right then, as he contemplated the contrast between his rough paw and her slim body, she seemed delicate to him.

But he knew that she wasn't.

He said, his voice barely above a whisper, yet still too loud in the quiet room, "The first thing he told me was that Karen had died."

Her mouth tightened, her eyelids flickered. He watched a single tear escape the corner of her eye and track a gleaming path along her temple, into her hair.

"I didn't even know she'd been sick. She'd sent me letters and I never read them. And Gus wrote, too, along with coming to try and see me every week. But how could they tell me what was happening when I sent their letters away with the trash, when I wouldn't talk to him, or even see him. I saw everything then, when Gus told me Karen was gone. I saw the sheer, mean, small-minded pride of cutting everyone off the way I'd done. The stupidity of it. Of all of it."

She put her hand over his, on her chest. He turned his over. Grabbed on and held tight.

"Gus said to me, then, 'You need to stop being stupid. You need to think, while you're in here, what being stupid ever got you but trouble and loneliness. You need to get past it, you hear me?' I nodded. I whispered how sorry I was, about Karen. I was pretty choked up. Gus said, 'Prove that. Do it by respecting her memory, by taking my visits from here on in.' I did, from then on. He never missed a visit. And after that, I even let myself be glad to see him."

Marnie sat up. She turned and came down to him,

her body pressing close to his. She lowered her mouth and kissed him. A long, slow kiss, as with her hand, she caressed him, over his chest. And down.

When she touched him, he groaned and wrapped his arms around her, good and tight, easing her over, onto her back, so that he had the top position. He took control then.

She put up no resistance or argument, made no move to take the lead. When he eased himself between her thighs, she was wet and eager. Ready. He saw desire in her eyes, saw the clear blue softened to the color of a summer sky. As he moved inside her, he looked down into her flushed face and almost wished that this thing between them could go on and on. She was a fine woman. The very best.

He wished he didn't have to lose her in the end.

But then he let go of the wishing, the hoping. He lost himself in the feel of her, so strong and soft, in her scent that was fresh and musky at once, like apples and rain and sex, all somehow perfectly blended together. She cried out his name.

He answered by whispering hers.

When he got up to leave after midnight, she watched him dress, her eyes low-lidded but still shining through the darkness of the bedroom.

She said, "You could just stay here, if you wanted. I would like that, if you stayed."

He shook his head. It was better to go, to hold the line at least a little, to keep reminding himself that no matter how great it was with them, it wasn't like they were taking it anywhere beyond the next few weeks.

In the end, she would return to that small town in California where she'd been born and raised. And he would go back to life as he'd always known it.

When he bent to brush a last kiss across those fine, full lips of hers, she said, "Saturday night, Gabe and Mary are having a big party out at their ranch." The Lazy H was really Mary's ranch, inherited from her first husband. Gabe had helped her fix it up—both the land and the house. Before Mary, Gabe was seriously into the player lifestyle. But now he was living the country life with Mary and her two-year-old daughter, Ginny—and apparently loving it, too. "I want you to take me," Marnie added, just in case he didn't know already what she was leading up to.

He knew about the party, had gotten the invite along with everyone else in the family and any number of Gabe's and Mary's friends. Mary, who wrote freelance, had put together a family cookbook and the party was to celebrate the cookbook's publication.

Marnie wrapped a hand around his neck, holding him near, not letting him escape. "Jericho."

"What?"

She spoke slowly, deliberately, as if there was something wrong with his hearing. "Will you go with me to Mary's party?"

He pulled on her arm until she let go of his neck and then he straightened above her. "I'm backed up with work. I've got bike orders waiting. The bike for the auction has taken up more time than I should have let it."

She refused to leave it at that. "Sorry you're overworked. So will you go with me Saturday?"

He thought about Ash, the previous morning, jumping all over him for messing with Tessa's sister. He just didn't want to get into it with the family over what was going on between him and Marnie. He didn't want to see worry and disapproval in their eyes. He'd had enough of that in the bad old days. "I saw the family last weekend, at Bravo Ridge."

"Some of the family, yes. And that doesn't answer my question." She spoke softly, the way he did, when he was angry.

"Look. I told you. I've got work I have to do."

"As in, no, you won't go with me?"

"What do you want me to say? This thing is between us. I like you. Okay, I more than like you. I'm flat-out wild for you, to tell it like it is. But it's not like we have to get the family involved."

"I don't get it. Last night, you ordered me to come to the charity ball with you."

"Yeah. And maybe we ought to rethink that."

"You don't want me to go to the charity ball?"

"Well, I just mean, we don't have to go together. We'll see each other there."

She looked at him for a slow count of five. Then she turned her head away. "Good night."

The next day at the shop, he kind of expected her to come looking for him.

Most of the morning, he was down in the main shop, working on the auction bike with the help of Big Jake and a couple of the other builders. The charity chopper was almost ready to go to the airbrush artist, which would finally leave him free to play catch-up with a couple of important projects for good customers that he'd left on the back burner for the sake Ash's auction.

Zoe, his baby sister, was there that morning, too. She'd brought her cameras, both still and video. Zoe was twenty-five. She'd been to more than one college but never graduated and had yet to hold down a job for any length of time. She had some serious talent as a photographer, though, and she was keeping a record in pictures and video of the creation of the charity-ball chopper.

As he worked and his sister took pictures, he kept thinking he would look up and Marnie would be standing there beside Zoe, waiting for him to get a free moment. Maybe she'd drag him upstairs to his workshop, with Zoe and Big Jake and the others standing right there watching, and make him kiss her senseless before she would let him get back to work. She would tell him she understood if he didn't want to take her to Mary's party or be her date for the charity thing, and she was willing to let that crap go.

But she never appeared. Zoe left at about eleven. She reminded him about the party at Mary's before she took off. He made noncommittal noises. A few moments later, he glanced through the window to the front office and saw her in there chatting with Marnie. Marnie said something and Zoe laughed. They seemed to be really hitting it off.

Marnie went to lunch with Gus. He found that out when he wandered up front at noon, kind of thinking he would ask her if she wanted to get some food with him. Little Ted was there, watching the counter. He said that Marnie and Gus had gone to eat.

Jericho went back to work.

Around two, he went out in front again. She was there that time, as expected, working the counter, ringing up a sale. The customer had a little boy with him. She asked the customer if he wanted anything from the gift area. The kid's eyes lit up. The boy ended up with an SA Choppers T-shirt, a skullcap and an SA Choppers keychain with his name on it.

Jericho watched the whole transaction. She was really good, he had to admit. Not pushy, just friendly and professional and offering the customer a chance to add a little cool theme merchandise to his bill.

He stood there, at the end of the counter, feeling edgy and out of place, waiting for her to ring up a second sale. He knew she must have spotted him by then. He was kind of hard to miss. But she never once acknowledged his presence.

Then Gus came out of his office. Marnie turned and started in with him about the SA Choppers Web site, how it wasn't up-to-date and she needed to get with the Webmaster, add the new merchandise she'd ordered, get some specs and pictures of more recently built choppers up on there.

"Especially the auction bike," she said. "There should be a section about that. We could put it up now, show pictures of the bike in progress and then, as soon as it's done, some shots of the finished product."

"So call him. Tell him what you want, say I'm good with it, that you're in charge of getting things current on the site." Gus turned around and went back in his office, shutting the door behind him. Probably in hopes she wouldn't follow him in there with more stuff she wanted updated or improved.

When she turned Jericho's way again, her eyes slid right past him. There was another customer at the counter. She went to take care of him.

By then, Jericho was tired of waiting for her to admit that he was standing there. He went back out to the shop and went to work. For the rest of the day, he did a pretty fair job of forgetting she existed.

He stayed at SA Choppers until after eight that night. There was plenty of work waiting. And as long as he concentrated on that, he didn't have to think about how she probably wouldn't welcome him if he showed up at the guesthouse, about how it looked like this hot thing between them was over after two nights.

Eventually, he went home, stopping on the way to get a couple of burritos and a six pack. He ate the food and drank three of the beers. And then he stayed up half the night mindlessly watching television, trying not to think about where he wished he was.

Saturday was a half day at SA Choppers. They closed the counter and the front end at noon. In the back, the builders could stay if they had stuff they needed to keep working on. Jericho got there at 5:00 a.m., long before anyone else. He worked by himself until seven-thirty, when Little Ted and Gus showed up. At nine, Marnie arrived to take over the counter from Gus, who'd opened up. Jericho knew she was on time, because he kept an eye out for her appearance through the sliding window that separated the front end from the shop.

She was looking for him, too. He knew because he caught her at it, checking through the sliding window at the same time he was, glancing away fast when their eyes met. That brought him a little thrill of satisfaction, to know she wasn't as uninterested as she kept trying to pretend.

About then he decided he'd had enough of this crap. It wasn't like they had forever, after all. Their time together was seriously finite and she had wasted a whole damn night that they might have spent together, sulking over his not being willing to take her to Mary's damn cookbook party.

Uh-uh. He was done with playing this game. He was having it out with her and he was doing it now. He put away the tools he'd been using and washed the grease off his hands. And then he went up front, where, for once, there was no one at the counter and she was sitting behind Desiree's desk, doing some damn thing or other at the computer.

He marched over to the edge of her desk.

At least she had the grace to admit he was there. She tipped her head back so she could see him from under the bill of her hat. "What?"

"I want to talk with you."

"Oh. Well. Right now, I'm working. I have a break at—"

He put up a hand. When she stopped talking, he went over and tapped on Gus's door.

Gus called, "It's open."

So he stuck his head in there. "Can you handle the counter for a few minutes?"

"Sure."

"Great. We won't be long."

"Hey." Gus showed him those perfect white teeth. "Take your time."

Marnie was already on her feet.

Jericho said, "Up to my workshop. Now," and walked right past her without stopping or glancing back to see if she followed.

She did. They went through the main shop and up the steel stairway.

He indicated the daybed when they got to the top, offering a seat. She shook her head, so they ended up standing by his drawing table, staring at each other.

Down below, it was suspiciously quiet for a moment. But then someone got to work pounding metal and an ancient Led Zeppelin song started playing.

She just stood there, looking at him, her chin aimed high and her eyes shooting blue sparks.

He rubbed the back of his neck. "Look…" He let the word draw out. Most women would take over talking if a guy just made a noise or two.

But Marnie wasn't most women. She kept on glaring at him, her arms at her sides. She didn't say a word.

"What do you want from me?" There. He'd asked a question. That ought to do it.

But she only pressed her fine lips together and shrugged.

Okay, he had no idea how to proceed with her. "I'm sorry, all right? I didn't mean to hurt your feelings."

She lifted her chin a fraction higher. That was all.

"Or piss you off," he added, just in case it was more that than the other.

She still refused to move or speak.

He stepped in closer, to see if she'd flinch back. Of course she didn't. She wasn't going to give him the satisfaction. Because he was there, so near to her, he sucked in a slow breath through his nose. Clean as rain, fresh as apples. Hey. If she wasn't going to speak to him, at least he could have the pleasure of smelling her.

A long moment elapsed. He breathed her in and she stood there staring up at him, refusing to move or to speak, her face cold, closed to him.

And that, her coldness, that really got to him. She'd been mad at him and scared of him. She'd laughed with him and yelled at him. She'd shed a tear for him when he told her about Karen's death. And she'd crawled all over him, moaning, driving them both crazy.

But never, until that moment, had she ever shown him a cold face.

That cold face infuriated him—had the blood buzzing in his veins like a hive of freaked-out bees. That cold face spurred him.

And he went too far.

He lifted a hand and flipped the bill of her hat by launching his middle finger off his thumb.

The hat jumped off her head and dropped to the floor. Her hair, loose now, fell around her shoulders, crackling with static.

She spoke then, at last. "That was just really rude." Her voice was low, carefully controlled.

"I'm a rude guy."

"I'm going now." She bent, scooped up her hat and headed for the stairs.

"Marnie."

She stopped without turning. He knew, absolutely, by the set of her shoulders, by the proud, stiff way she carried herself, that this was going to be it. If he didn't do something to make things right, it was over with them.

He wouldn't get those few weeks with her. He would get nothing from her beyond cool politeness and a distant glance.

And that seemed…impossible. And wrong. Way wrong.

It hurt him, just to think of it. And from now on, he'd better stay aware of what he really wanted here, better cut the crap and keep his eye on the prize.

Because he wanted those weeks. He wanted them real bad. Enough that he was willing to do what he had to do to make sure he got them.

"Marnie, will you be my date to Ash's damn charity ball? And will you let me take you to Mary's party tonight?"

She turned back to him then. But her face was blank, giving him nothing.

He went all the way. "Please."

Only then, at last, did she allow him a nod. "Pick me up at six tonight."

"I'll be there."

She nodded again. For a moment that felt like a knife slicing in, all the way to the heart, she stared at him intently. He dared to think she might stay awhile, that they could talk—*really* talk, not just throw angry words into the echoing space between them.

But then she seemed to shake herself. She whirled away and disappeared down the stairs.

Chapter Nine

That evening, Marnie half expected him to be late—
or even not to show. She wasn't completely sure that
she *wanted* him to show.

No. That was a lie. She did want to see him. But she
was angry with him. She wanted a hell of a lot more
from him than he'd given her that afternoon.

When he got there right on time, she was more than
little surprised. She kept her expression carefully com-
posed as she opened the door to him and she spoke with
little inflection. "Come in, please."

He did what she told him to do, stepping warily over
the threshold. "You look good," he said in a careful
tone.

She'd chosen her skinny pants, red platform peek-
aboo heels and silk blouse with care. "Thanks." He

looked good, too. Freshly shaved in new jeans and a nice shirt. But she didn't compliment him. Right then, she was in no mood to start trading admiring remarks. "Want a beer?"

"I'm thinking we should probably go."

"Go." She made a face like the word tasted bad.

"Yeah. Go. Isn't that what you wanted? To go."

"All of a sudden, you can't *wait* to get to Mary's?"

He stuck his hands in his back pockets and looked at the floor. "You're still pissed at me."

She remembered the hard things he'd revealed to her the other night and her resentment faded a little. "I'm just confused, I guess. You don't want to be seen with me—but you can't stay away? What's that about? It doesn't seem like anything good."

He lifted his head then and met her eyes directly. "I got no problem being seen with you. I'm proud to be seen with you."

"Coulda fooled me."

He rubbed the back of his neck. "It's the family, okay?"

"What about them?"

"Listen. Do we have to go into this now?"

"Yeah, I think we do."

He turned away from her and seemed to be looking out the glass door, toward the pool. Or maybe toward the main house. At least when he spoke, he did it clearly so she had no trouble hearing every word. "You know how it is in a big family. Somebody has to be the problem child, the one who never gets it right. In my family, we don't have a lot of losers."

She cut in strongly, "You are not a loser."

"No. What I am is an ex-con. That's about as far from 'right' as a guy can get in a family like mine."

She stared at his broad back and the remnants of her fury with him shriveled up and crumbled to dust. She only wanted to wrap her arms around him, only wanted to speak up on his behalf, to point out how great he was doing now, to tell him he should move on, leave the past behind, that she really did believe his family already had.

Instead, she asked, "You think they'll judge you, is that it? That they'll be after you, on your case, for getting involved with me?"

He turned back to her then. "Ash already has—on both counts."

"But you worked it out with him."

"We called a truce. That's not what I would call working it out. And as for the rest of them, I don't know what they'll do. And maybe that's it. I don't *want* to know what they'll do. Or what they'll say."

She held his gaze and spoke gently. "Well. I guess I do get it."

His green eyes softened. He scanned her face. "You do?"

"Hey. I ran all the way to Texas to avoid dealing with whatever reaction my family might have to my breakup with Mark."

"Uh-uh. Wait a minute. This is different. You know that."

"All I'm telling you is that my parents surprised me. They were sympathetic. Even my interfering grandpa was okay with it. I see now that they love me and accept me and I can stop making up stuff in my head about the way they think of me."

"Running away because some idiot dumped you is not the same as going to prison for grand theft auto."

Cautiously, she put up a hand.

He glared. "What?"

"We need to get something clear here. About Mark?"

"What? That you're still in love with him? I know that."

She spoke more softly. "What I was going to say is that Mark is not an idiot."

"I know that, too," Jericho said bitterly. "Mark's a nice, normal, solid, stable guy."

"He is, actually."

"But he also dumped you. And that makes him an idiot in my book."

Well, all right. That was very nice to hear. She wanted to grin—but she didn't. "On second thought, you have a point. Mark *was* an idiot for dumping me. But otherwise, he is the most un-idiotic person I know."

He shrugged. "Can we get back to the *main* point here?"

"Of course."

"You have to admit that your situation and mine aren't the same."

"No. They're not. But *you* have to admit, there are certain similarities."

"Yeah, all right. We both have family issues. Yours are mostly in your head. Mine are real."

She only looked at him. Patiently.

He started on about Ash again. "Look what happened with Ash. He got right on my ass when he heard that I spent the night with you."

"Only because my sister pushed him into it and Ash will do anything for Tessa."

"He still doesn't like it. He made that all too clear. He thinks I'm taking advantage of you in your…emotionally weakened state."

She braced her fists on her hips. "Do I look to you like I'm in a weakened state?"

"No, not to me. Not anymore. But apparently, to Ash, you do."

Was she offended? Not really. So far, she hadn't shown Ash a whole lot of mental competence. "Give him time. Ash'll get over it. And if he doesn't, well, that's his problem, not yours."

When he spoke again, it was without anger or bitterness. "You make it all sound so…workable."

She sent him a sideways glance. "As in, who knew Tessa's crazy sister could be so reasonable?"

A smile was trying to lift the corner of his mouth, although he didn't quite let it. Softly, he echoed, "Yeah. Who knew?"

They spent maybe twenty seconds just looking at each other. She thought how she liked his straight eyebrows and his mouth that usually looked grim but occasionally curved in a way that was all the more attractive for being so reluctant. She thought how she really would like to kiss him. After all, she had been more than a little worried that they weren't going to work this problem out, that she would never kiss him again.

He said, "When you look at me like that, I get hopeful. I get the feeling you're going to forgive me for being an ass."

"I get that feeling, too." She narrowed her eyes at him. "But don't you ever mess with my hat again."

He put up a hand, palm flat. "I swear. Never again."

"Well, all right, then."

They gazed at each other some more. Funny, how just looking at him got her hot. She thought of the things they had done together night before last, and the night before that. She thought, again, of kissing him. His kisses were magic. They set her on fire. She thought about skipping Mary's party after all.

He must have been thinking along the same lines, because he said, "We should go now. Or we'll end up finding something better to do…"

She knew he was right. And as much as she wanted to pick up where they'd left off Thursday night, she didn't want to miss the family party. Especially not considering that she'd almost broken it off with him for refusing to go with her.

So she grabbed her purse off the coffee table and gestured him out the door ahead of her.

The renovated ranch house at the Lazy H overflowed with people.

Party guests spilled out onto the wide front porch. People stood chatting by the porch railing. They sat in the row of white wooden porch chairs. And when the porch itself couldn't hold them all, they perched on the steps. They called out greetings as Jericho and Marnie emerged from one of Jericho's custom cars. He passed the key to a cowboy who was playing valet.

Marnie took his arm. "I'm really glad we came."

He didn't say anything, but he did glance down at her

with a look that almost seemed affectionate. And then he laid his big hand over hers, a fond sort of touch. Anyone who glanced their way would know they were together.

Marnie felt really good about that.

Jericho's half sister, Elena, was sitting in a white wooden rocker not far from the steps. Elena had long, thick brown hair threaded with gold and red and big golden-brown eyes. She waved as they climbed the steps. "Hey, Rico."

He stopped long enough to introduce her to Marnie.

"Glad you made it," Elena said. "Everyone's here. All our brothers and sisters. With their wives and their children and more than a few in-laws, not to mention a large number of family friends."

Mary Bravo greeted them at the door. "Jericho, I'm so happy you came." She told Marnie how pleased she was to meet her, then took her hand and led her over to a table stacked with copies of the newly released *Bravo Family Cookbook*. A sign on the table read Take One. "I want everyone in the family to have a copy." Proudly, she handed one to Marnie.

Marnie admired the cover. It was charmingly done. The green-and-white checked design framed a sepia-tinted picture of the ranch house at Bravo Ridge. Inside, it was ring-binder style, so you could add or remove pages. Marnie flipped through it, exclaiming over the great photos of the Bravo family. Tessa was in several of the pictures.

"Your sister provided more than one recipe," Mary said, turning for the door again where another late arrival had just appeared.

The cookbook covered a wide range of different foods and cooking styles. Everything from how to roast a whole pig in a barbecue pit to the world's best tuna casserole to duck with raspberries. As Marnie flipped through it, she spotted Jericho in a couple of the group pictures, sitting at dining room tables with the rest of the Bravos. She thought he looked way too serious and maybe a little uncomfortable. There was one, at Christmas in the dining room at Bravo Ridge, where he smiled. But it was a forced smile, a *say cheese* kind of smile.

"Zoe took all the pictures," Jericho said from close behind her.

She could feel the warmth of his big body so close, and his breath stirred her hair. Desire whispered through her. "I can't believe Mary's giving these away."

"I think that was Gabe's idea. He bought a couple hundred of them to pass around when Mary told him she wished she could give a copy to everyone who contributed."

"Did you contribute?"

"Are you kidding? No one in the family escaped Mary's nagging to be part of it. I'm in the barbecue section. It just so happens, I grill a mean burger."

Marnie was staring at a mouth-watering photo of sliced herbed prime rib. "Now I'm getting hungry." She set it back on the table, figuring Jericho would pick up his copy on the way out.

He already had hold of her hand and was pulling her toward the kitchen. She laughed and let him drag her along, loving the feel of his strong fingers wrapped around hers.

In the big kitchen, with its country-white cabinets and wood and granite countertops, there was food on every available surface. They grabbed plates and filled them, then moved on to the dining area, which was serving as the beverage station. They got a couple of beers and went out on the back patio to eat.

Tessa and Ash were out there. Jericho tried to go the other way, but Marnie nudged him with her elbow.

"What?"

"Let's sit over there, with Tessa and Ash. They have room at their table."

"I don't want any trouble."

"I'm sure Ash doesn't either. Come on…"

He didn't look happy, but he did follow her over.

"Can we join you?" she asked with a bright smile for both her sister and Ash.

Tessa beamed right back. "Absolutely."

Ash's expression gave nothing away. "Why not?"

Marnie and Jericho took the empty seats.

Tessa went on beaming. "I'm so glad you two made it," while Ash made a low noise that could have meant anything.

Marnie, smile firmly in place, sent Jericho a glance. "We wouldn't have missed it for the world."

Jericho almost choked on a forkful of hot German potato salad, but after he managed to swallow, he threw in, deadpan, "Yeah. We've been really lookin' forward to it."

Marnie said how great the party was. Tessa agreed with her.

It was awkward. And it might have stayed that way. But Marnie and her sister were both on the same page with this. They wanted the rift between the brothers mended.

Tessa asked Jericho how the bike for the charity auction was going. He relaxed when he started talking about his work. And then Ash seemed to lighten up a little, too. He said that he'd seen Zoe's video footage and he really liked the way the chopper was turning out. By the time Marnie got up to get another beer, Jericho and Ash seemed well on the way to healing the breach caused by the confrontation Thursday morning.

Jericho caught her hand as she rose. "What do you need? I'll get it."

From the corner of her eye, she read Ash's thoughtful expression and her heart lifted. Maybe he was finally realizing what a great guy his brother really was—considerate, tender and kind.

"Just a beer," she said. "And I can get it. You want one?" At his nod, she asked Ash. He nodded, too. Tessa wanted another glass of lemonade. "Be right back," Marnie promised as she turned for the kitchen.

The kitchen was packed with people, the door to the dining room blocked with guests sipping tall drinks, chatting and nodding. Marnie went around through the living area—and collided head-on with Zoe, who appeared pretty much out of nowhere, moving fast.

"Oops," Marnie caught Jericho's baby sister by the shoulders to steady them both. "Sorry, I…" The apology trailed off. She looked in Zoe's big blue eyes and saw they were brimming with tears. "What's happened? Zoe?"

But Zoe only sniffed and wildly shook her head. "I'm so sorry. It's nothing. Really." She dashed at her wet eyes as she pulled free of Marnie's hold and whirled to go the other way, toward the stairs to the second floor, practically at a run.

Marnie trailed along after her, muttering "Excuse me, sorry, excuse me" as she eased her way through the press of guests in the living room. Even though Zoe was obviously upset, they all let her go with no more than a concerned or puzzled glance.

Not Marnie. Yeah, she had a feeling she should probably stay out of it. But then again, well, maybe she could help. And nobody in the immediate Bravo family was nearby to go see if Zoe needed a little support.

At the top of the stairs, Zoe detoured through the first open door, shoving it shut after her.

Marnie hesitated before knocking. Clearly, Jericho's sister wanted a moment alone. Plus, Jericho would be wondering where she'd wandered off to.

But then, it didn't seem right to just leave Zoe in misery. Before she had time to talk herself out of it, Marnie gave the door a quick tap, just in case what Zoe really wanted was someone to talk to.

The door opened a slit. One teary blue eye peered out at her.

Marnie suggested, "I was wondering if maybe you wanted…I don't know, a little company?"

Without a word, Zoe stepped back. Marnie slipped inside and shut the door after her.

The room—a bedroom—was nicely decorated, in sunny yellows and creamy white. The lack of personal items had Marnie figuring that it must be a guest room.

Jericho's sister dropped to the edge of the bed, whipped a couple of tissues out of a box on the nightstand and buried her face in them. "I've really got to do something," she sobbed. "This can't go on."

You do? It can't? Marnie thought the questions, but didn't say them. Instead, she approached and sat down next to Zoe. She'd never been all that good with crying women. This was more a job for Tessa, who had all the tender, interested noises down pat, who didn't feel the least uncomfortable grabbing people in loving hugs.

But Marnie was the one who was here. So she snaked an arm across Zoe's shoulders and pulled her close.

Zoe put up no resistance. She dropped her head to Marnie's shoulder with a ragged little sigh. "I know my father's really trying," she said in a tear-clogged voice, "to be a better person, to be more…understanding. To quit acting like he has the right to run our lives…" Zoe sniffled and dabbed at her nose.

"But…?" Marnie softly prompted after several seconds of silence had passed.

Zoe gestured wildly with her fistful of tissues. "He called me a…free spirit." She sobbed and pressed the wad of tissue to her face again.

Marnie didn't get it. "A free spirit? That's bad?"

Another tight sob. "Actually, it's his code name for flake."

"Your dad called you a flake?"

"Essentially, yeah."

Marnie remembered the other not-so-great stuff she'd heard about Davis, like the cruel, dismissive way he'd once treated Jericho. She knew that he hadn't been all that excited about Tessa and Ash getting together, either—not at the time, anyway. "What a jerk."

"Thank you, Marnie. I kind of thought so, too."

"And he called you a 'free spirit' just now, is that it?"

Zoe nodded against Marnie's shoulder. "Mary was talking to him about how much my photographs add to the cookbook, how hard I worked, getting them just right. And my dad throws his arm around me and squeezes my shoulder and says, 'Zoe's our free spirit.' He gives a laugh. I hate that laugh. It's a condescending, judgmental laugh, you know? 'Zoe's our free spirit.'" She repeated the phrase in a mocking singsong. "I swear, if he ever says that to me again…" She sighed and dabbed at her eyes.

"You'll what?" Marnie prompted gently.

Zoe waved a hand. "Oh, I don't know. I shouldn't be so sensitive, I guess. I mean, it's basically true, what he said about me. I *am* a free spirit, a free spirit in a *good* way—or I have been. Until the last year or so, when it's starting to get old. I've been to college. More than once. Dropped out every time. And I've never had a job I couldn't quit."

Marnie found herself thinking of her work at SA Choppers. It was the first job she'd ever had where she loved just being there every day. She only hoped, when she went back home, she could find something half as satisfying. She said, "I know this is stating the obvious, but what about your photography? Have you looked for some kind of position where you do what you really like doing—where you can take pictures?"

Zoe sagged closer. "I haven't, no. I guess I ought to. I ought to start looking for something that interests me, shouldn't I? Something that doesn't require a degree, but also something I can do without getting bored out of my skull."

"Yeah. I'd say a job you enjoy might help a lot." She suddenly thought of her own family. And that made her chuckle.

Zoe pulled back to look at her. "What?"

"It's just, well, families, that's all. My family takes forever to get that I've changed. When I was a kid, I was a wild little sucker. So I was the wild one in all their minds long after I'd settled down into comfortable, upscale tedium in Santa Barbara with the supposed love of my life."

Zoe tossed her wad of tissues toward the wastebasket in the corner. It went in without touching the rim. "I take it the upscale life in Santa Barbara didn't work out?"

"Nope. My true love dumped me."

"What a fool."

"I think so, too. But it's for the best. I'm learning that now."

Zoe's grin was slow and knowing. "So you like hanging out with big, bad Jericho, working at his chopper shop."

A strange tenderness washed through her. "He's big. But he's not bad. In fact, he's a good man. The best. And yeah, I really like working at SA Choppers."

Zoe held Marnie's gaze. "Are you falling for the family rebel?"

It was a valid question, one Marnie had no intention of answering. "This conversation is about you, not me."

"I only want to say that if that happened, I think it would be just great."

"Thank you."

"And you do make me think, you know? I'm starting

to get that it's not so much what my dad said that bothers me, it's that I know they all think I'm a total slacker. So when they say 'free spirit,' I hear 'lazy and unmotivated.' And that really bugs me. Because I guess I kind of am."

"A slacker? No, you're not."

Zoe let out a sharp laugh. "We know each other for like ten minutes at Jericho's shop yesterday and five more minutes right now. I don't think you're in a position to tell me whether I'm a deadbeat or not."

"You're *not* a deadbeat. I know this. You just need the right job. You need to build your confidence a little. Then when your dad starts playing those old tapes, you can just smile and blow it off. Or tell him without a lot of heat that you feel hurt when he says that stuff."

"It all sounds really good." Zoe said the words, but Marnie doubted she meant them because she was simultaneously shaking her head.

Marnie backpedaled a little. "Or forget the whole job thing if that's not what you want right now. You could just try and talk with your dad, try to get him to see that you don't appreciate the free spirit crap and you'd really like it to stop."

"It's not only my dad. It's all my overachieving brothers. Even my mother—who's the sweetest, kindest woman in the world, by the way—thinks I should either get a nice husband and have a bunch of babies, or find something else constructive to do with my life."

"You want a bunch of babies? Or a husband?"

"For God's sake, no—not now, anyway. Maybe eventually. In a few years, after I meet the right guy, settle down and all that."

"So about that job—or a little heart-to-heart with your dad?"

"I'll think about it, Marnie. I seriously will." She pressed her hands against her cheeks and let out a gusty sigh. "Thanks."

"Did I help?" Marnie couldn't hide her surprise.

"You absolutely did. I've actually stopped longing to punch my dad in the face. And my tears are almost dry—and about Jericho?"

"Yeah?"

"He's had some rough times. But he is a good guy. The best."

"I think so, too."

Zoe put on a warning expression. "Treat him right."

Marnie resisted the guilty urge to explain that she and Jericho were open-ended, just for now, nothing permanent. "I will," she said firmly. "I promise."

Zoe tipped her head toward the door. "You go on. He'll be wondering where you went. I'll fix my face and be down in a few minutes."

"You sure?"

Zoe nodded. "I'm fine now. Really."

Marnie found Jericho in the dining room. When he spotted her, he gave her a questioning look.

She made her way over to him. "Sorry. I got side-tracked, visiting with Zoe...."

He didn't say anything, only nodded as he reached out and guided her hair back over her shoulder. A simple touch. And an intimate one. It felt good, companionable. Tender. It made her breath get all clogged up in her throat.

Marnie knew in her head that they weren't forever.

But sometimes, when he looked at her the way he was looking now, she *felt* like they were, like she'd actually found the right guy for her when she really wasn't even looking—a good guy, a steady-hearted guy. A guy who'd taken a few hard knocks and gotten back up on his feet and gone on with his life.

But then she thought of Mark, of his kind face, his serious eyes. A few weeks ago, *he'd* been the only guy for her. And maybe this thing with Jericho really was just a rebound thing, something hot and bright and bound to fade.

"What?" he asked after a minute, his voice a rough caress.

She shook herself. "Beer, remember? We're here for the beer."

They got their beers and the lemonade for Tessa and went back outside, where the sky had darkened.

Someone had turned on heat torches, to cut the chill of the spring evening. They sat for a while, chatting with Tessa and Ash, and Luke and Mercy, too, who took seats at the table with them.

Little Lucas sat in his father's lap, drooping toward sleep as the grown-ups talked softly in the gathering night. Once or twice, Luke brushed the top of his son's head with a kiss. Marnie saw Tessa and Ash exchange a look and knew they were thinking that it wouldn't be long before they had their own baby to cuddle to sleep.

By ten, Jericho was ready to get going.

The party had been clearing out over the past hour. Luke, Mercy and Lucas had already left. Tessa and Ash, too.

Jericho and Marnie had stayed on. Surprisingly, he was enjoying himself. She seemed to be, too. They ended up on the front porch, sitting in the porch swing together, slowly swaying back and forth. Beyond the porch roof, the dark sky was thick with stars.

She said, "The land is so pretty here. I love the rolling hills, the oaks and fields of wildflowers we passed on the drive up. And the way the long grasses bend in the wind...."

"Yeah," he agreed. "The Hill Country is some of the nicest country in Texas. Gets good and dry in summer, though."

"Makes me want to take off my shoes and run around barefoot."

"That could be fun—as long as you don't step on a rattler."

She groaned and poked him in the ribs. And then settled in closer against his side.

He pressed his lips to her hair, sucked in a slow, deep breath of her rain-fresh scent. "You about ready to head home?"

"Hmm." She kept them swaying, one toe to the porch boards.

At this rate, they'd still be sitting on the swing when morning came. He eased his arm from around her shoulder and got up. "Come on..."

"This was fun." She let him pull her to her feet.

He wrapped his arm around her again—because he could. Because it felt good, to have her slim, strong little body tucked against his side.

Of course, she lingered in the kitchen, telling Mary what a great party it was, whispering with Zoe—over what, he had no clue. The two of them had their heads together like best friends for life or something. He just had her moving again when she decided that Mary should sign his copy of the cookbook.

So he got one of the few copies left on the living room table and Mary wrote "With Love and Thanks to Jericho" on the inside front flap and then her autograph beneath that.

Ten minutes later, they were finally on the road.

He teased her as they drove. "You got something big going on with Zoe?"

She turned her head and smiled at him, a dreamy smile. "I like her. We had a nice…talk."

"About what?"

She glanced away. "About her life and what she wants to do with it, I guess you could say."

He chuckled. "It's a woman thing, right?"

"Exactly. A woman thing—but if you could just not call her a free spirit, ever again, that would be helpful."

He knew then what must have happened. "My dad called her a free spirit and she got upset about it."

Marnie turned her head again to look at him, her chin tilted at a defiant angle. "Yeah. So, see? You're not the only one who feels like an underachiever in the Bravo family."

He grunted. "That supposed to make me feel better about being the family embarrassment?"

"You are not the family embarrassment and you're in control of how you feel about your place in the family."

"You sound like a shrink, you know that?"

"Hey. It's better than being in need of one—and I'm just pointing out that sometimes it's so easy to start thinking you're the only one. And then you find out the guy next to you feels just as lonely and left out as you do."

At the guesthouse, she closed the blinds and came into his arms. He kissed her and thought how great it would be if he never had to let her go.

But he did have to let her go, he reminded himself. And he would, when the time came.

He undressed her, right there in the living room, peeling the silk shirt off her, the lacy bra, the tight jeans and her little purple thong. She kicked away the red shoes.

And then she returned the favor, first getting down and pulling off his boots and his socks, then rising to deal with his shirt and his jeans. Until he was as naked as she was.

Slowly, he sank to his knees in front of her. He parted the tan curls and kissed her, easing her thighs wide so he could kiss her even more deeply, so he could run his tongue along her silky, wet, secret folds. Until she shuddered and collapsed over his shoulder, laughing and moaning at the same time.

He rose, lifting her with him, easing her down from over his shoulder, taking her nipple in his mouth. She threw her head back, fingers splayed in his hair, and let out a pleasured moan. And then she lowered her mouth to his and slid down his body until her face was below his and her ankles were firmly hooked around his waist.

She took charge, reaching down behind her, her sleek body bowing backward, to wrap her hand around him good and tight, to guide him into place. Once she had him in position, she flexed those strong thighs of hers.

With another long moan, she lowered herself onto him. He cupped her bottom, fingers sliding in, providing extra stimulation as she moved on him.

His legs went to rubber. But still, somehow, he remained upright, and she knew how to wrap herself around him, so her weight was evenly distributed, her legs and arms hooked securely in place. She held on tight enough for both of them.

He came first. But not by much. He was still spilling into her when she followed him over the edge.

And then she curled herself down close to him, tucking her head against his neck, licking him there, gently sucking his flesh against her slightly parted teeth.

It felt good.

So good…

He carried her into the bedroom. As he laid her down, she watched his face, her blue eyes glowing, soft with satisfaction, her smooth cheeks flushed. He thought again that he never wanted to lose her.

And then, again, he reminded himself that this wasn't forever. That he served a certain purpose in her life at a time when her world was changing. That he'd better enjoy every minute he had her with him, every touch.

Every soul-deep kiss.

And he would.

Oh, yeah. He would.

Chapter Ten

Monday morning, after Marnie got to work, Jericho came up in front from the shop. He went into Gus's office and shut the door. When he came back out, she couldn't stop herself from sending him a questioning glance.

He lifted an eyebrow, but volunteered nothing.

She didn't push him. They were getting along great, so she didn't worry that he'd been talking to Gus about her. If he had private business to discuss with his partner, she wasn't butting in on that.

Gus went home at lunchtime. He returned in a pickup, towing a flatbed trailer. She was sitting out on the stone bench under the sad pistache tree, drinking a Fresca, when he drove through the gate. She saw the gorgeous chopper he was towing and she stood up to get a look at it.

The bike was slightly smaller than the average, airbrushed in metallic pink and black, the chromed wheels in a blade pattern, the front end raked so fine, the handlebars not quite high enough to be your classic ape hangers, the whole thing so sleek and beautiful, it sucked the breath right out of her lungs. She was already walking toward it as Gus parked the pickup.

It was only up close and personal, leaning over the flatbed's railing, that she saw the small, pink, looped ribbon airbrushed on the fat, bobbed rear fender. The name was written on the ribbon a flowing script: Karen.

It was Karen McNair's chopper.

Marnie stepped back as Gus got out of the cab. "It's beautiful." She couldn't have kept the awe out of her voice even if she'd tried.

He skimmed off his skullcap and tossed it into the cab through the open side window. His bare head gleamed in the afternoon sun. "Rico says you want to learn to ride."

Her mouth dropped open. She could hardly believe what he seemed to be telling her.

Those black eyes of his bored right through her. "If I let you borrow Karen's bike, you will take excellent care of it."

"I will." She barely got the vow out through her clutching throat. "I swear I will."

"You will do as Rico tells you to do. You will not get ahead of yourself. No showing off, no hanging it out."

"I promise. I swear."

His gaze never wavered. "Goggle the horizon, angel." It was an old biker saying, one that originated with the Navy Seals. It meant *Keep your head up* and *Drive safely*.

"I will," she vowed again. "I will be careful. I will keep my head up."

And then he smiled his slow, amazing smile, the one that could light up the darkest room. "Well, all right, then."

Joy speared through her like a bolt of lightning. She let out a whoop and she threw herself at him.

"Whoa," he said, laughing, as he gathered her in, hugging her tight, spinning her around until she was dizzy with the pure joy of that most precious moment.

Gus had loaned her Karen's bike. She was deeply honored.

And she was going to learn to ride.

She started her lessons after work that day, in the SA Choppers lot.

Jericho took her through the long series of hand signals and told her where she could look them up online to memorize them. He told her she wouldn't be leaving the lot until she knew them all by heart.

Then they went through the primary controls and their functions: throttle, clutch, gearshift lever, front brake lever, rear brake pedal. She already knew them. But she listened anyway, with fierce attention, aware that Gus was keeping an eye on her progress through the windows at the front of the shop, as well as of her promise to learn what Jericho taught her and learn it well.

From there, they went on to the secondary controls: starter, cutoff switch, speedometer, tachometer, temperature gauge, turn signal switch, high/low beams, fuel supply valve, choke and ignition.

He showed her how to run a pre-ride inspection,

and the starting procedure, including proper mounting from the left side, with one hand holding the front brake lever. Then he let her start up the bike. Because the engine was cold, she used the choke.

Once she started it safely, they spent some time on clutch control. She learned to feather the clutch—to ride with it in the friction zone, partially engaged—for better control at low speeds.

That initial day, she was allowed to ride around the parking lot in first gear. By the end of that lesson, she could stay on and stay moving forward in a smooth, even ride, no stalling. And without lurching.

The next day, after Jericho had tested her on her hand signals and her mastery of the simple steps he'd taught her the day before, they moved on to shifting and the concept of countersteering as well as slowing into turns. By Wednesday, she was allowed out of the lot.

Thursday, she got up to speed on the big slab, aka, the interstate. And Friday night, in bed, after a long afternoon bike ride, they planned a short road trip to the Hill Country Sunday.

She really wanted to make the trip last two days, to leave on Saturday. But she still needed a dress for the charity ball, which was only a week away. So Saturday was designated a shopping day. Gus had let her take the half day off and she and Tessa were combing the department stores in the morning and then having lunch on the Riverwalk together afterward.

"I wish we could leave Saturday," she whined for the umpteenth time.

Jericho laughed. "It will be Sunday before you know it."

She stuck out her lower lip at him. "Not soon enough for me."

Idly, he rubbed the backs of his fingers along her cheek. "I guess we could leave Saturday afternoon, if you get back in time."

She stuck a fist in the air. "Yes! That is what I've been waiting to hear. And I swear, I will have that damn dress before noon, if it kills me."

"Well, okay, then."

"So that means we'll be staying in the Hill Country overnight?" She tried to keep her voice really casual. Really cool. Not to make a big deal out of it—even though it *was* a big deal.

If they stayed over somewhere, it would be their first time to spend an entire night together. He could hardly leave her bed at midnight if they were sharing a hotel room somewhere, could he?

And also, an overnight trip would mean more time on Karen's chopper. She really did love to ride, loved the roaring rumble of the engine vibrating up through her torso, loved the freedom of flying down the highway on two wheels, the sun on her shoulders and the wind coming at her, pushing, wrapping around her, resisting but not breaking her forward momentum.

Bikers called all enclosed vehicles the cage. She totally understood why now. There was nothing like the freedom of being on a big bike, the up-close contact with the outside air, the sense of power and self-determination, of direct connection to the road.

She rolled over and rested her folded arms on his bare chest, meshing her fingers, propping her chin on them. He touched her, a long, lazy caress. From the top of her spine, between her shoulder blades, and downward, all the way, into the low sacral curve and then up onto her right buttock. He molded the shape of it.

She tipped her head so it bumped his chin. "Did you hear me?"

"I heard you."

"Overnight, then?"

His hand started on a slow trip back up the way it had come. "We have a cabin up there, for the family's use. I'll see about getting the key and having the caretaker stock up the fridge."

"Oh, I am liking this. I am liking this a whole lot."

His hand slid under her hair to clasp the back of her neck. "You are, huh?"

"I am."

"Then show me some gratitude."

She scooted down his body, until her lips were within kissing distance of his growing arousal. "Oh, I'll show you a lot more than gratitude," she whispered, and proceeded to do exactly that.

Marnie found her dress at the first vintage clothing store Tessa took her to.

It was red, with an empire waist and thin straps that tied behind the neck. In the back, it had laces. The skirt was gored, full but not *too* full. And it had tiny beads sewn into the red overlay fabric, beads that glittered when she moved. Her bare shoulders and arms looked smooth and sexy in it. Plus it made her look fuller in the bust than she really was.

Tessa said, "Wow."

And Marnie smiled in smug satisfaction. "That was

a whole lot easier than I expected." The price was right, too. Only sixty bucks. She had room in her budget for sparkly red high-heel evening sandals, and an antique-look choker necklace with garnet-red stones. The choker had earrings to match, so she bought those, too.

Tessa already had her dress, but found some really nice earrings at Nordstrom's that would look great with it. And they had lunch, as planned, on the Riverwalk at noon.

Marnie told her sister about the thrill she got riding a chopper and about the bike trip she and Jericho were taking to the Hill Country that afternoon. "We're staying overnight," she said, beaming like a kid on her way to Disney World. "At the family cabin, Jericho said."

Tessa seemed to be studying her. "You look so happy."

"Well, I am."

"No. I mean, *glowing.* I don't think I've seen you this happy since…" Tessa frowned. "Come to think of it, I don't think I've *ever* seen you this happy."

Marnie set down her glass of iced tea and picked up a triangle of sandwich. "What? Is that bad?"

"No, of course not. It's just, well, is this getting serious, between you and Jericho?"

Marnie swallowed the bite of sandwich. It went down hard and dry. "No. It's wonderful. Beautiful. But we've both agreed it's nothing serious, nothing permanent."

Tessa leaned closer across the small table they shared. "Agreements change."

Marnie waved a hand, trying to be casual and easy— but almost knocking over her glass of tea. "Oh, I don't think so. I think, when the regular office person comes back from maternity leave, I'll be heading home to California, the way we planned."

"We?"

"Me. You. Remember? I did promise you that I wouldn't stay forever."

Tessa said, "But you *could* stay forever. I would love it if you stayed."

Marnie saw Jericho's face, suddenly, the grim set to his sexy mouth, the strong brow, the deep, watchful green eyes. She heard his voice again, heard what he'd told her the first night they made love.

But I like it on my own. I'm not up for any long-term thing, not into settling down.

He always left her in the middle of the night. And she'd yet to even see the house where he lived….

"Marnie?" Tessa was frowning at her, a frown of sisterly concern.

She reminded herself that she *was* having a fabulous time. And just because her love affair with Jericho had an expiration date didn't make it any less than exactly what she needed right now. Plus, they'd only been lovers for a week and a half, certainly not long enough for her to start spinning fantasies about forever.

Most likely, her irrational yearning for a more permanent relationship with Jericho was simply part of the process of getting over a big breakup. She was transferring her feelings for Mark onto Jericho. She needed to stop that. She needed to remember that Jericho was her hot rebound guy and she was fine with that.

And besides, he *would* be staying the whole night with her. Tonight.

"I'm all right," she said, and pretty much meant it. "Though now and then, I just wish…"

Tessa leaned even closer. "What? Tell me."

Marnie sat up straight and shook her head. "No. Nothing. I like things just the way they are. Temporary. And terrific. I wouldn't change a thing."

Marnie was ready when Jericho picked her up at the guesthouse at three.

She wore jeans, boots, a T-shirt and a denim jacket she could tie around her waist. She also had a fanny pack that carried the barest essentials: driver's license, cash and a toothbrush.

They drove to the shop, where they switched from his car to the choppers. He locked up the chain-link gate and turned the alarm back on behind them and they were on the road.

In no time, they were out of town and on the open highway, heading north, the land that rushed past them swiftly changing, growing greener as they rolled deeper into the Hill Country. It was a little late in the season for the famous Texas bluebonnets. But still, there were plenty of wildflowers to enjoy—whole fields of them, in yellow and purple, white and delicate pale blue.

They stopped in Fredericksburg for a while to check out a museum there and grab a cold drink. Jericho told her that Fredericksburg and much of the Hill Country had been settled by immigrants of German descent.

Next, they detoured over to Luckenbach, which was hardly more than a couple of weathered barns and some picnic tables tucked under the shade of old oak trees.

Jericho said that one of those barns was where Willie Nelson used to play with Waylon Jennings.

After Luckenbach, Jericho took her to the family cabin, which was a few miles north of Fredericksburg, down a dusty driveway, in the middle of a gorgeous field of wild grasses and flowers. The cabin was simple on the outside, of unpainted pine. Inside, it had everything to make their stay comfortable: a modern kitchen, an attractive living area. And a bedroom with a big, wide bed.

The caretaker had been there and stocked the fridge with food. They took a couple of beers out to the blue-painted bentwood chairs on the front porch and sat for a while, talking about the shop, about the new suppliers she'd lined up to manufacture the merchandise for the gift area. And about the welder's art. Jericho claimed a workday wasn't complete if he hadn't fired up his welder's torch at least once.

He asked the important question. "So, did you find the dress you were looking for?"

"I did."

"Then you're all ready for the ball, huh?"

"That's right. What about you? Got a tux?" she asked, just to watch him look horrified at the very idea.

But he surprised her. He pointed the mouth of his longneck her way. "As it happens, I own a tux. I may be the troublemaker of the family, but I still have to put in appearances at black-tie events now and then."

"I'll bet you look super-hot in it."

"You can decide for yourself about that next week." He drank from his beer. "Hungry?"

She shook her head. "Let's ride some more."

They put on their helmets and climbed on the bikes. He took her down past Kerrville and through Bandera and then north again through Boerne. She loved every minute, every mile of that ride.

When they returned to the cabin that time, it was after eight. Her backside was aching and her bones kept rattling, even after she climbed off the chopper and had both feet firmly planted on solid ground. Not that she was complaining. Choppers had a hard ride and Karen's bike was no exception. A chopper was built for style and speed. It wasn't that agile on turns. And if you wanted comfort, you should get yourself a touring bike.

Jericho fired up the gas grill behind the cabin and grilled them some steaks while she poured a bag of spring-mix lettuce into a wooden bowl and added tomatoes and avocado. They ate. She hadn't realized how hungry she was until she took the first bite.

He laughed and said he liked a woman with an appetite.

She had an appetite, all right. For a nice, thick steak. And then for him.

They made love fast and hard. And then again a while later, much more slowly. She drifted off to sleep content on every level, thinking that the past afternoon and evening had been about as perfect as any day could get.

Jericho watched her sleeping.

She hugged her pillow and a slight smile curved her lips. Probably dreaming of rolling down the highway on Karen's chopper. Funny how she took to riding. Like a fish to water, like a bird to the wild blue yonder.

And she wasn't like a lot of women, just wanting to ride along. She was no fender bunny.

Uh-uh. She had the spirit of a true biker, a passion for the art of motorcycling. It was going to be real hard to say goodbye to her.

But he would.

It was three weeks since she started working for him. And three weeks until her temporary job at SA Choppers was over and she returned to California. Three weeks until The End.

That was how he'd started thinking of it. As The End.

It would be way too easy to get attached to her. But that wasn't going to happen. It was all going to go down as planned. As agreed on.

Which was fine. Good. Just the way it ought to be. He didn't know why his mind insisted on wandering into forbidden territory, on daydreaming about what it might be like if she stayed.

Probably because three weeks seemed like much too short a time. The End was coming at them way too fast.

She sighed and snuggled deeper into the pillow. A silky-straight lock of her hair fell across her mouth and then fluttered with each breath. He reached over and smoothed it back. The feel of her skin against the pads of his fingers was magic to him. Just that small, light contact got him turned on again. Only a touch, and he wanted to wake her, to make love to her again.

But no. He wasn't going to do that. He was going to leave her the hell alone and let her sleep.

Flopping over to his back and lacing his hands

behind his head where they wouldn't be so tempted to reach for her, he stared at the shadowed ceiling. He probably shouldn't have brought her up here to the cabin in the first place. The main point was supposed to be not to get too attached, not to do stupid things like spend a whole night in the same bed with her.

But here he was, staying the night.

He'd done a boatload of stupid things in his life. Enough that he'd let himself believe that he'd been stupid in every way possible. Not so. Lately, a whole new meaning of the word was opening up for him.

Stupid over a woman. Stupid over Marnie Jones.

Marnie Jones, who still loved a nice, normal citizen of a guy named Mark.

She insisted that Mark was not an idiot. And if Mark was not an idiot, chances were he would be back around to try and work things out with her.

Jericho was loving every minute of this ride they were on together. But he had no illusions. She would go with her old boyfriend when he came to get her. And if the boyfriend didn't come, she would go anyway.

She moaned in her sleep. He glanced over as she rolled from her side to her stomach. She grabbed the pillow again, whispered a name.

Not *his* name.

"Mark…"

Chapter Eleven

Marnie woke up alone.

She had that moment of complete disorientation. The night-dark room, the bed, all of it was strange to her. She had no idea where she was.

And then everything swung into focus. She remembered: the cabin, the two glorious rides through the Hill Country....

Jericho.

They'd made love. She'd fallen asleep beside him. This was a big night, their first whole night together. The first time they would wake up in the morning in the same bed.

And how was that going to happen if he was gone?

She sat up, tamping down the sudden swirl of unhappy emotions: worry, anger, hurt. It might be a big deal to her, the whole-night-in-the-same-bed thing. But that didn't mean it had to be all that significant for him. They didn't have that kind of relationship, the kind where greeting the morning together was an important link in the chain of caring, another step toward commitment, a proof of their growing closeness.

They were supposed to be living in the moment. She wished her foolish heart would stop trying to make the moment into something more.

She threw back the covers. "Jericho?"

No answer. She listened. Heard the faint songs of night birds outside, through the half-open window.

She got up. "Jericho?"

Quickly, she checked the bathroom, the living area, the kitchen. All empty. She started for the door—and then realized she was naked. So she detoured back to the bedroom to get something to put on.

His T-shirt was there, tossed on a chair, tangled with hers. His boots waited on the floor with hers, one tipped on its side, a sock dangling out.

Her mood lightened considerably. If he'd left, he would have put on his boots at least.

A pair of white terry-cloth robes hung from twin hooks on the back of the bathroom door. She put on the smaller one and went out through the main room onto the front porch.

Out there, the night birds' songs were louder. Clearer. The three-quarter moon silvered the hills and gave a muted blue luster to the chrome on the two choppers waiting in front of the porch. She turned her head toward the small round table and the pair of blue chairs and saw him, a darker shadow among shadows, sitting in the far chair.

He didn't say anything.

Neither did she.

But her heart felt suddenly lighter inside the cage of her chest. She went to him, not making a sound in her bare feet. Taking the other chair, she gathered her feet up and wrapped her arms around her knees.

He moved, reaching out. Offering her a sip of the beer in his hand.

She lowered her feet to the rough boards of the porch and took the bottle. Tipping her head back, she put it to her lips and let the cool, bitter taste slide down her throat. She set it down on the table between them.

"I always liked it up here," he said after a moment, his voice low and velvety-rough. "My dad bought this land back in the eighties, when we were kids. We used to come camping up here, the whole family. This cabin wasn't much more than a shed back then. We'd bring tents. And sometimes horses, from the ranch. Those were good times, simple times."

He fell silent. She looked over and saw him pick up the beer and drink the rest. He bent to the side and put the empty on the porch floor by his chair on the far side. Then he turned her way.

She knew he was watching her. His eyes shone at her through the night.

He said, "Coming here makes me remember that it wasn't all bad, growing up a Bravo. I might have been a misfit, but sometimes I *was* happy. Now and then, I even felt like everything would be all right." He reached out his hand toward her.

She met it with hers, her fingers curving into his waiting grip. His thumb traced the line of her wrist, back and forth, bringing those warm little flares of erotic sensation, of promise.

He gave a tug. She came up out of her chair and over to his, sinking down to him, turning sideways so her bare legs hung over to one side, dangling above the boards of the porch floor. He bent and slid the beer bottle back against the wall behind them, out of the way of her feet.

When he straightened, she touched his jaw— beard-rough, warm—and then palmed his cheek, learning the feel of him anew, there in the dimness of the middle of the night.

He whispered, "Say my name."

It seemed an odd request. Still, she happily obeyed. "Jericho," she said against his waiting lips. "Jericho, Jericho…"

He kissed his own name right off her lips.

She said it again. "Jericho. It's a very sexy name."

"You like it?"

"I do." She framed his face between her hands, kissed him some more. Slow, lazy kisses, tender and deep.

His eyes opened to meet hers. "My mom chose my name."

"It's so…biblical."

He laughed, a low, sexy sound. "We all went to Bible school, when I was a kid. I learned there that Jericho is where the Israelites ended up when they returned from bondage in Egypt, led by Joshua, successor to Moses."

"Like I said, biblical. And your mom chose the name for you because...?"

He shrugged. "She said once that she liked the way it sounded. And we've all—at least the boys in the family—got biblical names. Asher, Gabriel, Luke, Matthew, Caleb, me. I'm not sure about Travis, though. Is Travis biblical?"

She laughed. "Like I would know—and have I met Travis?"

"He's not around all that much." He touched her lower lip with his thumb, rubbing a little. It felt so good, his touch. It always did.

She confessed with a sigh, "I was named after a character in an Alfred Hitchcock movie. Marnie was a beautiful compulsive thief. In the movie, Sean Connery plays the guy who loves her and marries her and helps her find out why she is the way she is." She didn't mention that Sean Connery's character's name was Mark, though she and Mark used to joke about it, back in the day. "I always hated that my mom named me after a disturbed woman who steals anything that isn't nailed down and hates the color red—oh, and she's frigid, too. Did I mention that?"

He was grinning, showing even white teeth. "You did steal my chopper."

"Only to make a point."

"I thought it was to get even with me for saying rotten things about you."

"Partly, but to make a point, too."

"What point was that?"

"That I still had a spark, an edge. A wild side."

He widened his eyes in mock terror. "That was somehow in question?"

"It was. Yeah. It was."

"But not anymore."

"Uh-uh."

"What about the color red?"

She thought of the killer dress she'd bought for the charity ball. "I happen to love red, as a matter of fact."

"Unlike Marnie in the movie."

"Right. And I am *not* frigid."

"You need someone to testify to that? I'm there for you, Marnie."

"Good to know. I mean, just in case I ever feel the need to prove it in court."

"Forget court." His voice had that certain wonderful roughness, that ragged heat. "You can prove it right now...."

She whispered, "Again?" Though she didn't need to ask. After all, she was sitting on him. She could feel him, feel the hard, thick ridge of him, pressing against her, beneath the fly of his jeans.

He answered, low, on the verge of a groan, "Yeah. Again."

She slid off his lap. He seemed to know exactly what she meant to do. The top two buttons of his jeans were already undone.

He ripped them wide and pushed the jeans down enough to free himself. "Come here. Here to me…" He reached for her, his hands clasping her waist.

She came back to him, straddling him. She had nothing on beneath that robe and her body knew him so well now, welcomed him. It was a simple thing. Perfect. Smooth.

He slipped inside, pushing so deep. The robe settled

around them, providing privacy they didn't need in that isolated place.

Her soft cries filled the night.

The next day they shared a late breakfast. Then they rode on up to Austin, where everything was lush and green. And the traffic was bad, even on Sunday. He insisted that they visit Barton Springs, in Zilker Park.

He said, "You haven't been to Austin if you haven't seen Barton Springs."

It was a pretty sight, a huge natural pool fed by an underground aquifer, the water clear and so inviting. They paid the three-dollar fee, each, so they could take off their boots, roll up their jeans and stick their feet in.

Jericho said the water was the same temperature, sixty-eight degrees, year-round. The pool was packed in the summer, but people swam there in all seasons. There were lifeguards on duty that day—and every day, Jericho said. And there was a bathhouse with changing facilities and a gift shop, too.

For lunch, he took her to another landmark: Old No. 1, the original Threadgill's on North Lamar, home of good Southern-fried cooking—and famous as a birthplace of the early Austin music scene. They had fried pickle spears and seafood po'boys while the jukebox blared classic tunes—including a certain bump-and-grind song, "You Can Leave Your Hat On."

She grinned at the sound of that, remembering it from that funny nineties movie, *The Full Monty*, about unemployed working guys in England who became strippers to bring in some cash.

When the song started playing, she sent Jericho a glance. He was already looking her way, waiting to catch her eye.

They both started laughing. She knew he was thinking what she was: of how she'd made him promise never to mess with her hat. She asked the guy behind the bar who the singer was.

Before he could answer, Jericho said, "Tom Jones."

She raised her bottle of root beer to him out of pure respect, she was so impressed.

Then they got back on the bikes and rolled down through the Hill Country, taking their time, stopping in at the cabin again for a while, sitting out on the porch in the blue chairs, drinking ice water and enjoying the warmth of the day and the way the wind made the wild grasses ripple and wave.

Around two, they headed for San Antonio, where they went straight to the shop to put the bikes away and switch to the whip again. By then, Marnie was kind of considering it a weekend created to indulge her every fantasy.

Which was why she lured him into the empty building, grabbed a hat from the merchandise display and then dragged him upstairs to his workshop. There, she had her way with him on the daybed, wearing the hat, which she strictly forbade him to touch.

Afterward, he held her in his big arms and sang that song they'd heard at Threadgill's. He sang a little off-key, but he knew all the verses, which surprised her.

And made her laugh.

It was after five when he dropped her off at the guesthouse. She asked him if he wanted to come in. He shook his head and kissed her one more time. She got out of the car and gave him a wave as he backed out of the driveway.

And then she went inside and filled the tub and sank into it with a grateful sigh, groaning only a little when she turned her backside to the power jets and let them beat away the stiffness from spending most of the day on a chopper. She rolled up a towel and used it for a pillow, settling back and closing her eyes, letting the events of the past twenty-four hours play through her mind, reliving every moment of the weekend's free-wheeling, hard-jarring ride.

It had been a great time.

The best…

Her cell rang. It was in reach, right where she'd set it, on a small wicker stand by the tub. The sound startled her. She'd been kind of drifting off to sleep. Water sloshed over the edge as she shot to a sitting position.

The ringing continued. She swiftly dried her hand on the towel she'd used as a pillow and answered without checking the display.

Big mistake.

It was Mark. "Marnie. Don't hang up."

Chapter Twelve

Her pleasure—in the hot bath, in the tired, sore, sexually satisfied state of her body, in the beautiful weekend just past—it all evaporated.

Mark. Why? She drew her legs up and wrapped her free arm around them tightly. "What is it? Is something wrong?"

"Marnie…"

"Marnie, *what?*"

"I… How are you?"

"Tell me what this call is about or I am hanging up."

"It's…nothing."

"Nothing. You're telling me you're calling me for nothing. Nobody died. No one's in the hospital. There's no blood and no fire. Nothing."

"I just...I miss you, you know? I come home at night and the house is so empty. I don't like it. I want—"

"Stop. Don't. I'm sorry you're unhappy. But it's just...It's not my fault."

"I know. I know it's not. I only...I want to know that you're okay."

She let out a slow sigh and reminded herself not to engage. There was no point in getting into it with him. He had to know that as well as she did.

Still, the yearning in his voice did affect her. It hurt. It hurt terribly that he seemed to be suffering. She had to school her voice to an even tone. "Look. I asked you not to call me. You said you would leave me alone."

"I know I did. Just five minutes."

"Mark."

"Three, okay? Three."

She drew another slow, steadying breath. "Talk, Mark."

"Fine. Okay. I think I made a big mistake. I was an idiot. I'm seeing that now."

She might have laughed if she didn't feel so much like crying. An idiot. He admitted that he was an idiot. And after she'd defended him so staunchly to Jericho, insisting that he wasn't one.

"Mark. You said it wasn't working out, remember? That you weren't happy. That I wasn't what you wanted, that we didn't want the same things. And that you were worried about me. You were afraid I'd lost touch with my real self, my wild side."

"I didn't know what I was talking about."

"Yes, you did. And you were right."

"It had been a rough time, at work." Mark was a hotshot at Santa Barbara's biggest ad agency, a driven man. He was *always* having a rough time at work because he was killing himself to get ahead. "I lost touch with what matters, that's all. I said things I shouldn't have…."

"No. You didn't. You said what needed saying. I thank you for that."

"What do you mean, you thank me?"

"Come on. It's too late. You have to see that."

"No, Marnie. I don't. I don't see that at all. Listen, I know what you want, I know what you've always wanted. And I'm ready now, I swear it. Marnie, let's get—"

"No." She cut him off before he could say it. "Don't you dare, Mark Drury. It's too late and you know it and now you're feeling bad about it. Well, get over it. Please. Get over it and move on. Find someone who's right for you."

"Marnie. I'm begging you. Listen, I—"

"Mark, I have to go now. I'm hanging up. Don't call me anymore."

"Marnie—"

She made herself disconnect, although his voice, calling her name so desperately, echoed in her ear.

And then, with a furious cry, she hurled the phone against the far wall. It made a hard smack as it hit and then dropped to the floor. Probably broken—which was okay. Fine. Mark had bought it for her, after all. It was still on his cell phone plan.

She needed to get herself her own damn phone.

Marnie let the phone lie there all night. The next morning, she went to toss it out and found that it wasn't broken. Not even chipped.

She threw it in the trash anyway.

And that day, on her lunch break, she went out and bought herself one of those pay-as-you-go phones. Fifty-five bucks for a whole month of unlimited minutes, including texting. Then she called Tessa, her mom, her dad and her grandpa and told them to use the new number.

Her grandpa wanted to talk. No surprise. She told him about her temporary job at SA Choppers and how she loved it, about how she'd learned to ride a chopper.

He shouted, "Maybe you're gonna be settlin' down there in Texas."

Even though he'd yelled it, she found it hard to believe her grandpa, who thought everyone should live in North Magdalene, would suggest such a thing. Stay in Texas? She had to admit that the thought held a certain appeal. She could work at SA Choppers for the rest of her life and not get bored. And the thing with Jericho...

Well, she knew it wasn't going to last forever. But she sure wouldn't mind if it went on longer than just the three weeks that remained until Desiree came back to work.

But no, she reminded herself. She really was a California girl at heart. When Desiree came back, she would go home, pick up the pieces, figure out what she wanted to do next with her life.

"Oh, Grandpa. I'm only here for a while. Of course I'll come home."

He went on as if she hadn't spoken, just the way he always did. "Tessa would love that, you stayin' right there in San Antonio," he yelled. She held the phone away from her ear in order not to cause eardrum damage. "I mean, what with that new baby coming and all. A woman needs blood family around her. And it sounds like things are goin' good for you there."

"Grandpa, I—"

"Never say never. It's all I'm tellin' you."

She gave in and promised she wouldn't say never. After which he launched into a long-winded update, filling her in on what was happening with every one of her North Magdalene relatives. She had a lot of relatives and his update took a while.

Finally, she had to cut in. "Grandpa, I—"

"…and then Gina told me I had to be more patient with those boys and I said, 'Don't talk to me about patience, woman. If Brady and Craig don't start behavin' themselves, I can't be responsible for what I might—'"

"Grandpa!"

"Eh? What? You say somethin', gal? You speak up now, you hear?"

"Grandpa, I need to get back to work now!"

"What? Work? Well, why didn't you say so? Okay, then. You take good care of yourself and your sister, and I'll be talkin' to you later." He said goodbye and hung up, which made her smile. Her grandpa would blather on for hours. But he'd never been one to prolong a goodbye.

She made it back to SA Choppers in plenty of time. The first thing she did when she got there was enter her new phone number in the employee database. And when Gus appeared, she wrote the number down for him personally, so if he needed to reach her, he could.

Then she called Jericho up in his workshop. He didn't answer. Probably had the welding torch going, with the rock and roll up good and high. She left him a message, telling him again what a great time she'd had that weekend, adding her new phone number at the end.

He called her about five minutes after that. "Just checking to see if this new number works. How about tonight? Six. We could ride for an hour or two."

She said yes before he finished asking her.

They rode until eight. In the deepening darkness, he followed her on his chopper to the guesthouse. She cooked a quick dinner for both of them and then took him to bed.

It was so good, to have his big hands on her. When he was touching her, she could forget everything: Mark's desperate, lonely voice on the phone, her fast-approaching return to California, where she had no idea what she was going to do with herself.

Everything. All of it just…faded away. There was only the heat of him, the tenderness, the pleasure he brought.

She must have fallen asleep afterward, because she woke up from a dream where she was trying to tell Mark, again, how it was over. Really over, and she didn't want to see him.

When she opened her eyes, Jericho was getting dressed, moving silently in the dark bedroom, already in his jeans, but still barefoot, his T-shirt gathered on his big arms as he straightened them overhead.

"You're going…" she whispered. She didn't mean to sound wistful—but she supposed that she did.

He dropped to the edge of the bed, the T-shirt still wadded, trapping his arms. And then he swore, a very bad word. He shoved the T-shirt down his arms and tossed it to the floor.

She sat up and reached out, laying a tentative hand on his back, between his shoulder blades, right over the beautiful eagle tattoo. "What? What's the matter?"

He turned his lowered head to glance her way. "You been thinking about Mark a lot lately?"

She blinked. And she knew her face had gone bright red, though maybe the room was dark enough that he couldn't see the flush flooding upward over her cheeks.

He said, "Tonight's the second time you said his name in your sleep."

She groaned. "Oh, God. At the cabin…?"

He grunted, turned his face away from her again—and nodded. "I gotta tell you. I understand, but still. It's kind of a turnoff, you thinking of another guy when you're in bed with me."

"But I *don't*. I swear I don't. When you're touching me, there's no one. No one in the world but you…"

He laughed, a low, ironic sound, and shook his head. "Marnie. You say his name in your sleep."

She shoved the covers back and swung her bare feet over the edge, so she was sitting beside him. "I've known Mark since I was nine."

"What? That's supposed to make it okay?"

"No, no of course not. But most of my life, he was there, you know? At the cabin, I was dreaming of when we were kids, of something that really happened once. Mark slid down a hillside covered with shiny-leafed bushes and ended up in bed for two weeks with a really bad case of poison oak. In the dream, I was trying to call to him, to warn him to watch his step…" She couldn't help it. She had to reach out again. She brushed her hand down Jericho's heavily muscled arm.

And her heart gave a glad little lurch when he let her take his hand.

He said, "You got to admit. A shrink would have a field day with that dream."

"Maybe. I don't know. But I do know I'm never going back to Mark, that it wasn't right between us."

Do you? That little voice in her head challenged. *Do you really know you'll never go back?*

She tuned out the voice, put it firmly on *ignore*.

Jericho turned her hand over, lifted it, sank his teeth gently into the fleshy pad at the base of her thumb. It felt so good, she had to swallow a moan.

"And tonight," he said gruffly. "What were you dreaming about tonight?"

"I don't remember exactly. Mark was yelling at me. I was begging him to leave me alone."

"*Did* he leave you alone?"

"It was all pretty fuzzy. I woke up with no…resolution, the way it usually is in a dream."

"Marnie. Come on. Give it to me straight."

She realized then that she wasn't going to be able to just forget about Mark's call yesterday. It wouldn't be right, to leave Jericho in the dark about what was going on. Even if her relationship with him had a time limit on it, it still mattered to her. *He* mattered. A lot.

"Okay," she said. "I don't know why I dreamed about him when we were at the cabin. But as for the dream tonight, well, he called me yesterday, after you dropped me off. He asked me to try again with him."

Jericho pulled his hand free of hers. "And you said?"

"I said no. I said I wanted him to leave me alone. I said it very clearly. And then I hung up."

"Did he believe you?"

"Give me your damn hand back, please." She spoke through clenched teeth.

He shocked the hell out of her by doing just that.

She laced their fingers together and held on tight. "I have no idea what Mark believes. What he said is that he's having second thoughts, having trouble accepting that it's really over between us, that he..." She almost faltered. But no. It was better, just to get it all out. "...that he wanted to marry me."

Jericho said nothing for a moment. And then, finally, bleakly, "Marriage."

"Yeah. It's pretty incredible that he'd do that, actually. When we were together, I wanted to get married and he was always putting it off."

"Maybe he's seen the light."

"Yeah. Right."

"Maybe he doesn't believe you really mean it when you tell him you're through with him."

"But I do mean it. And I told him so, repeatedly. And then I hung up. I don't see how much clearer I can make it." She clutched his hand, hard, against her belly. "So. Can we forget about Mark now?"

"I can. I don't know about you." He spoke flatly, but when he turned to her, she saw that the ghost of a smile haunted the corner of his mouth.

She whispered, "What I do know. What I have zero doubt about, is that there is no man in the world I would rather be with right this minute than you. There is no man who does for me what you can do. There is no man, ever, who has given me so much pleasure. Such fun. Such...honesty. And such a damn fine time—all of it. Every minute with you is the best minute I ever had." *I wish it could go on forever,* she thought, but didn't quite have the guts to add.

He said, "You sound like you mean that."

"Because I do."

He hooked his free hand around the back of her neck and pulled her close to him. "I guess I can hang around here a little while longer."

"Now you're talkin'," she whispered, as he covered her mouth with his.

After Marnie told him about the ex's phone call, about how the guy had begged her to take him back, Jericho knew it was only a matter of time before Mark Drury showed up in San Antonio. As he saw it, the only way that *wouldn't* happen was if she left for California first.

The End was coming much too fast.

Jericho thought about how they should maybe call it quits now, that she probably could use a little time without him in her bed every night. Time to figure out what she really wanted. Time to have her answer ready when the ex showed up to plead his case.

Yeah. Jericho thought about that.

But he didn't break it off with her. Screw the ex. Jericho had three more weeks with her. He wasn't volunteering to give up a single day. Marnie would have to make that call.

She didn't. She came to work as usual Tuesday morning and he was in her bed Tuesday night. They took the choppers out for long rides after work twice more that week. He was having the time of his life and she seemed to be enjoying herself, too.

Saturday morning, he and Gus drove the charity-ball chopper over to the five-star hotel where the big party was being set up. The ballroom was packed with catering people and organizers from the Texas State Endowment. Up on the stage at one end, technicians were doing sound checks and moving equipment around.

His mother was there, which he'd expected. Aleta Bravo was born with a silver spoon in her mouth and a Junior League membership card in her hand. For this event, she would be representing the sponsor, the family company, BravoCorp.

She'd always had eyes in the back of her head. Maybe that came from raising nine kids and living to tell about it. She spotted them about forty seconds after they entered the ballroom. And she came right for them, weaving her way toward them through the crowd of setup people, his sister Zoe and a couple of Blue Hairs in tow.

The Blue Hairs were charity ladies who worked for the Endowment. Zoe was there to set up her little slide show that went with the bike. His mother hugged him and then hugged Gus. She introduced them to the Blue Hairs. Finally, she turned them over to Zoe, who showed them the back entrance where they could roll in the chopper, and pointed the way to the high circular display stage smack in the center of the room. The chopper, as it turned out, was the auction's main event.

He saw all the other auction stuff, a lot of it pretty pricey-looking, arranged on tables that rimmed the ballroom, and felt a little sick to his stomach. Yeah, he'd joked with Marnie and Ash about getting six figures from some philanthropist with a yen for the wild side and very deep pockets. But come on. What were all these rich society types going to care about an SA Choppers bike?

Then again, it was a little late to worry about that. He rolled the bike up the ramp, put the stand down, hugged his baby sister and he and Gus got the hell out of there.

Ash had ordered a stretch limo for the night.

The six of them, Ash, Tessa, Jericho, Marnie, Gus and Gabriella Santiago, the airbrush artist who also did all the shop's graphics, would be going together. The long, black car waited in front of Ash and Tessa's house when Jericho, Gus and Gabriella pulled up in Jericho's whip. The limo driver gave them a wave as they started up the front walk.

Ash answered the door. "Tessa's still getting ready and Marnie's still in the guesthouse. Drink?" He led them into his study and poured Maker's Mark.

He offered a toast. "Here's to a better-than-average rubber chicken dinner."

"I'm for that," said Gus, raising his glass, too. Gus was looking exceedingly smooth that night in a shadow-stripe tux. And Gabriella was stunning, as always, her long black hair flowing halfway down her bare back, her dress the changeable blue of peacock feathers.

Jericho drank and set down his glass. "I'll go check on Marnie, see if I can move things along…."

She was on the path that wove around by the pond when he went out the back door, wearing a red dress that skimmed her slim figure and sparkled in the fading light of day. She had her hair up, with little curls of it loose against her slim white neck. When she saw him, she smiled and then twirled around on the walk, holding the skirt out—Cinderella in red.

He went to her.

She whistled and gave him the once-over. "You look so hot. I could do you right here by the fishpond."

"You know, I was thinking pretty much the same thing about you."

She put her hands on his shoulders and her little red bag tapped him on the back. And then she lifted on tiptoe to brush a quick kiss against his lips. When she stepped away again, he offered his arm and they walked side by side to the back door.

Tessa was coming down the stairs when they got to the front of the house. Her long velvet dress was a deep green. Jericho thought she was almost as pretty as Marnie.

Ash came out of the study and went to kiss Tessa and whisper something in her ear. She flushed and gave a happy laugh.

"I think we're ready," Tessa announced.

Ash nodded. "The limo's waiting."

They sat at one of three big tables reserved for the family, close to the stage.

Jericho felt good, *really* good, to have Marnie at his side. She was smart and fun and beautiful. And, for that night and a little while afterward, she was with him.

He also felt good about Gus, felt that he had done his mentor proud. When Gus took him in after he got out, he had nothing to offer but a willingness to work and a talent with the machines he loved. Now, as SA Choppers' reputation grew because of the bikes he built, Jericho actually saw that he was giving a little back to Gus, that together, they were building something that neither could have managed alone.

And then there was the chopper he'd created for tonight. In the center of the ballroom, up on its own private stage, that machine looked amazing. Gabriella had outdone herself with the paint. The bike was a study in metal-shot gold and amber, with touches of turquoise blue. It looked like a giant hornet, or maybe a mythical creature from some whacked-out druggie's twisted nightmare, sleek and dangerous, shining in the spotlights, ready to roll.

Maybe not the kind of machine anyone there that night would fork over serious bucks to claim. Maybe making it the centerpiece of the evening had been a mistake.

But looking at it shining up there, Jericho almost didn't care if it brought in a big chunk of change or not. He was so damn pleased with the way it had turned out, with the way it looked under those bright lights.

After the main course, when the waiters ran back in again bearing dessert, the lights went down. Screens dropped from the ceiling, one on each wall.

It was time for Zoe's slide show. Jericho tried not to groan.

But then, as it turned out, it was fine. It was good. It was *really* good. And not so much a slide show after all. Zoe had made a damn movie about SA Choppers, about the bikes that they built—the one in the middle of the ballroom, in particular. There was good music, loud and hard with a driving beat. And there was a clear thread-through, a little background on Jericho and Gus and Gabriella, too. And the story of the building of a special bike.

He looked across the table at his mom and dad while Zoe's little movie played—looked, and then looked again. He couldn't believe what he was seeing.

Tears shone in his dad's eyes. Jericho blinked to make sure his own eyes weren't playing tricks on him.

But no. It was real. His dad glanced away at first, trying to hide the emotion. But then he gave it up. He turned his head back and stared straight at Jericho. He gave a slow nod.

And Jericho saw that it had come out all right between them after all. He had Davis Bravo's respect.

More important, he was learning to respect himself.

Zoe's movie ended and the lights came up. He put his arm around Marnie. She leaned in close to him and he breathed in the rain-and-apples scent of her hair.

She whispered in his ear. "That was really good. And the bike turned out so fine. I have a feeling you might get those six figures."

He chuckled. "We can hope."

They'd gotten some senator to play master of ceremonies and auctioneer. Since the auction was a silent one, where people wrote their bids and their auction numbers on the sheet of paper by the item, the senator's job was to charm everyone and spend a while delivering pitches about each of the prizes.

Once that was over, there was dancing. Jericho held Marnie in his arms and thought about how he would take that red dress off her as soon as he got her back to the guesthouse.

He joked with his brothers. He told Zoe she was a genius and she hugged him and said she was so glad he liked the movie she'd made. And he carefully avoided ever glancing at the auction sheet mounted beneath the chopper in the center of the dance floor.

They closed the bidding at 1:00 a.m. And at one-thirty, the senator got back up on the stage. He pointed out the table by the door where the row of smiling ladies would be only too happy to take the winners' money. And then, lowest to highest, he announced what each prize had brought.

It took a really long time. Too long, in Jericho's opinion. He and Marnie kept shooting each other will-this-ever-end glances. More than once, he saw her hide a yawn behind her hand.

The bike was last, which was a hell of a relief to Jericho. At least it had brought in the most.

"*Stinger,* by Jericho Bravo of San Antonio Choppers, airbrush art by Gabriella, is our top prize of the night," the senator shouted. "Dax Girard of *Great Escapes* magazine claims our featured offering with his butt kickin' bid of one hundred and fifty thousand dollars. That's right, folks. One hundred fifty thousand! Let's hear it for San Antonio Choppers and for Mr. Dax Girard!"

Chapter Thirteen

They had to hang around through the photos for the society rags, for pictures of Gus, Jericho and Gabriella alternately shaking Dax Girard's hand in front of the auction bike, the senator beaming in the background, and Dax's beauty-queen date trying to sneak into the frame.

Jericho had heard of Dax, although this was the first time he'd actually met the man. Girard was the heir to the kind of fortune that made the Bravo money look like chump change. He'd spent years adventuring all over the world. And then he'd started *Great Escapes,* a glossy travel magazine.

Dax collected all kinds of vehicles. If Jericho had known that Girard was going to be there, he probably would have been less worried about how much the

chopper would bring. It was Girard's kind of thing—
meaning it had a powerful engine and it was one-of-a-
kind.

They didn't get back to Ash and Tessa's until almost
four. Ash suggested a nightcap and they all filed in for
a last drink.

Jericho was just realizing he was going to have to
take Gus and Gabriella home before he could get
Marnie alone. But then Gus and Gabriella said goodnight and headed for the door without him. Jericho
trailed after them.

On the front step, Gus tipped his head toward the
limo driver still parked at the curb. "Ash had the
driver wait. You go on back to the lady in red. We've
got a ride."

Jericho grabbed him in a bear hug. "What a night,
huh?"

"You did good, son," Gus told him softly before he
turned and started down the walk, his hand at the small
of Gabriella's back. She glanced back and gave Jericho
a wave and then she smiled at Gus. Gus pulled her a
little closer. They'd had a thing once, a few years ago.
Watching them now, Jericho wondered if maybe it was
still going on.

Gabriella was a fine woman. And she and Gus
looked really good together.

When he turned around, Marnie was waiting. She
held out her hand. He called goodnight to Ash and
Tessa and they went back through the house, past the
bulldog sleeping in the corner of the kitchen, to the
white cat sitting by the glass door.

"Gigi, no," Marnie told the cat.

Tail high, the cat strutted off toward the family room. They went out, engaging the lock behind them.

In the guesthouse, he turned her around and untied the laces at the back of her dress. She held up her arms and he pulled it over her head.

They kissed. And then, before he could do more, she bent and untied his black shoes, slipping them off and then his socks after them. She made him take off his tux and fold it neatly over a chair.

"You're driving me crazy," he muttered. "You know that?"

She gave a throaty laugh. "That's pretty much the plan." And then, taking her time, she peeled away that tiny bit of strapless bra, the sexy little thong. And last of all, her red high-heel sandals.

Then, finally, she came to him. When he kissed her, when he took her down onto the bed, he tried not to imagine what it might be like.

If the two weeks they had left could somehow, magically, stretch out into forever. If The End never came.

But the two weeks that followed were nothing at all like forever. The days whizzed by faster than a world-class chopper, wide open on the big slab.

They worked. They rode in the evening. They spent every night together. By then, he wasn't even bothering to get up and go to his place while it was still dark. He wanted every moment he could get with her. He stayed at her side.

The next weekend came. They went to the cabin. They made love. They rode up to Austin again. They talked and laughed.

And then, all of a sudden, it was her last week. Gus heard from Desiree Monday. She would back the next Monday, right on schedule.

Monday went by and then Tuesday, every moment a pure pleasure. And then lost, gone, over way too fast.

Wednesday, Gus asked for a partners meeting at lunch. The two of them went to the coffee shop down the street.

Gus had his laptop with him. "Look at this." He turned the screen Jericho's way. "See that red line, the way it goes up at a roughly seventy-five-degree angle? That's our merchandise sales in the past five weeks, at the counter and through the Web site, which Marnie has seriously updated."

"Cut to the chase," Jericho said darkly, even though he already knew exactly where this was going.

Gus sent him a sideways glance. But then he went on without commenting on Jericho's attitude. "We can clear out that small storeroom on the other side of the front office for her. She can help Desiree at the counter and be our merchandising director. She'll be paying her own salary from the first. She has a knack for bringing it in. Within a year, with her working the gift shop and keeping the Web site current and fresh, I'm projecting eight thousand and change pure profit. That's the *first* year. She's already on me with ways to expand, ways to grow the profile and build name recognition. We do fine now. With Marnie Jones on board, we'll do a whole lot better than fine."

It sounded good to Jericho. Too good. He had to shut his mouth tight over the urge to give Gus the go-ahead, to say, *Sure, why don't you ask her what she thinks....*

He had to remember that this was not the plan. Marnie had stuff to do in her life. Marnie needed to go home, to have a long talk with that nice, stable boyfriend of hers, who had realized what a fool he'd been and only wanted her back. It wouldn't be right to try and hold her in Texas.

"No." He pushed the laptop back around so it was facing Gus. "Let her go," he said.

Gus stared at him. And then he shook his head. "I thought you were through with being stupid."

"I'm doing the right thing."

"The hell you are. You're being stupid."

"Gus. I'm not jacking around. Let her go."

Gus left it alone after that—left *him* alone.

Jericho knew his longtime friend was seriously ticked off at him. After their meeting at the café, Gus spent a lot of time in his office, with only his pit bulls for company.

Too bad. Gus would get over it.

And Marnie would go home.

Which was good. For the best. Jericho was absolutely sure of that.

Friday night, it all went to hell.

It was after they had made love and they were lying in bed. He had an arm wrapped around her and she rested her head on his shoulder. The world smelled of apples and rain and he was feeling good, satisfied, doing a decent job of keeping his mind from wandering off onto the subject of her leaving.

Which was coming up fast. The next day was her last at SA Choppers.

She said, "I've been thinking…"

He didn't like the sound of that. *I've been thinking*. It spoke to him of dangerous possibilities, of the clear chance that she would soon have him focusing on the very subject he was trying to avoid.

"I've done a hell of a great job at SA Choppers," she said.

He couldn't argue with that. "Yeah. You have."

"I have seriously crunched the numbers…"

He lay very still. As if by not moving, he could keep her from saying what she was going to say next.

Not a chance. Proudly, she told him what he already knew. "I've made back my salary in increased merchandise sales, did you know that?"

"Yeah. I know that." He ran a finger down the silky flesh of her arm. Maybe if he made love to her again before she went any further with this….

But she kept on. "I've been thinking that you guys could afford to hire me *and* keep Desiree."

"Marnie—"

She wiggled away from him enough to prop herself up on an elbow. "I'm serious. Think about it—I mean, don't just say no automatically. Really consider what I'm telling you. I love this job. I know we said—and I always just assumed—that I would go back to California once the job was over. But you know, I think I might as well stop kidding myself. I might as well go ahead and admit that I don't want to go. And if I can make money for you guys and enough to live on, too, well, everybody wins."

"Marnie. Come on. You can do better for yourself."

She rolled on top of him, caught his face in her two

soft hands and kissed him hard. "What are you talking about? Better? There is no better. I like it here. I *love* it here. Suddenly, I'm living the life I never let myself dream I could, the *right* life, for me."

"We planned—"

She shut him up with another hard kiss. "Listen to me. Plans change. And that's why I was thinking, you know, what if I…talk to Gus about it?"

He took her by the arms. "Marnie, you're not listening."

"Uh-uh. *You're* not listening."

"Marnie. No." He said it loud. And then he said it again. "No."

She stared down at him, her lower lip trembling. "Let go of me." He released her. She slid off him and rolled onto her back. A long, raw moment went by, where neither of them said anything. And then, in a near whisper, she asked, "Just like that? Just…no?"

"Marnie. It's not the right thing for you."

"You don't get to decide what's right for me. *I* get to decide that."

"Marnie, I…" he reached for her.

She only scooted farther away. "Don't. Just… don't, okay?"

The words were there, inside him. They pushed, hard, at the back of his throat, demanding to be said. *I love you. You're all I want. All I've ever dreamed of.*

But he didn't say them. She could do better. She *would* do better. He would see to that.

She had her head turned toward him, waiting.

He looked straight at her. And he spoke flatly. "It's a bad idea."

"Why?"

"You need to go back home, work things out."

"Work *what* out?"

No damn way he was mentioning that idiot's name. "Look. I told you I wasn't up for any long-term thing."

Tears brimmed in those big blue eyes. But she didn't let them fall. She drew in a shaky breath. "Oh. Right. I knew that."

He hated himself. But he was absolutely certain he was doing a good thing here. He sat up, pushed back the covers. "I'll go." He swung his legs over the edge of the bed.

She said, so softly, "Just like that, huh? You walk out. It's over and done?"

He didn't turn to look at her. Instead, he stared blindly at the far wall. "Yeah. Just like that." He was certain that would do it.

Not with Marnie. The bed shifted as she sat up. "I think you really should turn around and face me when you're dumping me."

He winced. "It's not like that. You know it's not."

"Oh, I think by now I should know when a guy is dumping me. Look at me," she commanded.

So he turned. He looked.

She sat very straight, the sheet drawn close to cover her perfect little breasts, her strong jaw set. "The truth is I already talked to Gus."

He considered that. Should he have known that she would? Probably. He shrugged. "And what did Gus say?"

"You know what he said."

"Tell me anyway."

"He said he'd already tried to talk you into hiring me, that he told you I could make money for you."

He refused to look away. "Hey. Money isn't everything."

"Gus said you told him no, and since you two are partners, you have to both be on board with it before he can hire me."

"That's right."

She made a sound. It might have been a laugh. Or something darker. "And you're not on board with it."

"No."

"But—"

"Marnie. No."

She went on anyway, in a small voice. "Even if you don't want to be with me, I don't see why I couldn't—"

"Stop. Give it up. It's a nonstarter. Forget about it. Go back to California."

The silence stretched on forever. Finally she nodded. "Well, all right. If that's how you want it, I'm gone."

So he got up. He put on his clothes. And he left her for the last time.

It had happened, just as he'd known it would. The End had finally come.

Marnie didn't get it. How could it be like this?

Somehow, Jericho's ending it with her was even worse than when Mark dumped her.

It made no sense that it should be worse. Mark had been her best friend. They'd lived together for years. She had believed that Mark was the man she would marry.

But still.

Losing Jericho was worse. Marnie felt like her heart

was breaking all over again, shattering into a thousand tiny pieces this time, never to be put back together again.

She tried to tell herself she was being ridiculous. She'd known all along that this would happen. Jericho had told her how it would be. She had agreed with him, made jokes about his being her hot rebound guy.

And really, some things just didn't last and that was the beauty of them. She needed to remember that. Sometimes a love affair was like a flower. It bloomed. And then it died. And the very shortness of its life made you appreciate it more.

The whole point had been that it was supposed to be temporary, a fling. But somehow, hardly realizing what she was doing, she had let herself start thinking forever. She'd had no right to do that. But she had anyway.

In the morning, early, she went over to the main house and told Tessa and Ash that she would be leaving the next day. Ash looked kind of stunned.

Tessa just took her hand and walked her back to the guesthouse. Once they were inside, she shut the French door and leaned back against it. "I wish you would stay."

Marnie shook her head. "No. Really. Gotta go."

"Did something happen with Jericho?"

"Nothing we didn't expect from the beginning."

Tessa did what she did so well. She held out her arms. Marnie went into them and held on tight.

When Marnie finally let go, she offered tea. They shared a cup. Tessa asked her to come back when the baby was born. Marnie promised that she would.

"And tonight, come over to the house for dinner?"

"I'll be there."

When Tessa left, the phone rang.

It was Grandpa Oggie. Marnie told him that she was heading home the next day.

Her grandpa chuckled over that for some unknown reason. He could be so annoying. And after that cackling chuckle of his, he shouted, "What's that they say? Home is where the heart is."

Was he getting senile? She couldn't help wondering. "Grandpa, I really have to go now. I have one more day of work left and if I don't leave, I'll be late. I'll see you Tuesday or Wednesday."

Her grandpa said nothing. Probably because he'd already hung up.

In spite of what she'd just said to her grandfather, she considered not showing up at SA Choppers after all. It *was* her last day. She doubted anyone would fault her for calling it quits a little early. Gus would understand. And Jericho would probably be relieved.

But no. She'd made a commitment to be there until Desiree returned. Even with her silly heart in pieces, she would keep her word on that. She was not going to collapse this time. Forget throwing everything in the car and running away. She would not go crazy.

She was stronger than that. *Better* than that.

At least she'd learned that much now.

Besides, it was only a half day. How hard could it be?

Too hard, as it turned out.

She spent the whole morning with her stomach in a knot and her mind on everything but work. She kept waiting for Jericho to show up in the front office. He never did.

At noon, as she was moving on autopilot, getting ready to check out for the last time, Little Ted appeared with a cake.

A goodbye cake. For her.

The other guys came up front, too. And Gus emerged from his office, followed by Chichi and Dave. The dogs stretched out on the floor behind the counter. And Gus made a little speech about how they would all miss her. Everybody started clapping. There were even whistles. And a catcall or two.

It was right then, while they were all clapping, that Jericho slipped in from the shop.

She was careful not to meet his eyes. She gazed blankly into the middle distance, pasted on a smile for the rest of them and said, "Thank you. I'll never forget you—not any of you. And when I'm gone you'd better get someone to dust the gift area, or I will come back and haunt you." She turned to Gus, who was looking at her so fondly that the shattered pieces of heart ached all the harder. "Can we cut the cake now?"

Little Ted stepped forward with a big knife. "Go to it."

She concentrated on that, on cutting the cake with We'll Miss You, Marnie in black icing on the top, and loading the pieces onto paper plates. The next time she glanced toward the door to the shop, Jericho was gone.

It's fine, she thought. It's best this way. I don't need to see him again. We've already said everything that needs saying.

They made short work of the cake. She got hugs from all the guys.

And that was it. Time to go. Gus gave her the envelope containing her last paycheck. "Come here," he said.

He led her outside, where Karen's bike was loaded onto a flatbed trailer.

She knew what was happening, she just couldn't believe it. "Gus, no. It's not right. I couldn't—"

He grabbed her in a hard hug. "Angel, you can. And you will. Karen would have liked you. And she never would have wanted her bike to end up stuck in the corner of the garage under a tarp." He took her by the shoulders and held her away from him. Those black eyes were shiny with moisture. "Goggle the horizon."

She blinked away tears and nodded. "I will. I swear it."

He followed her back to Tessa's, where he unloaded the bike and she rolled it into the garage, next to her car. And then, after one last hug, he gave her an envelope with the bike's paperwork in it. And he was gone.

In the guesthouse, she called U-Haul. They told her where to go in San Antonio to rent the small trailer she would need to haul her new bike back to California. And then she got out her suitcases and she started packing.

She had a stack of bras in one hand and fistful of thongs in the other when she realized that someone was knocking on the French door in the living room.

Jericho?

Just the idea that he might have come back, might have decided it wasn't over with them after all—just thinking of the possibility that it might be him—had the thousand pieces of her heart trying instantly to reassemble themselves.

Which was really, really dumb. Not to mention hopeless. There was no way that Jericho was going to suddenly change his mind about telling her to get lost. She dropped the underwear into the smaller of the two open suitcases and marched out into the living area.

It wasn't Jericho.

It was Mark.

Mark, right there at her door, in San Antonio, looking like any girl's dream of the perfect man, lean and tall, with dark hair and eyes to match. He wore a casual button-down shirt and jeans just faded enough to look worn, although she knew they weren't. He always paid a fortune for his clothes—jeans included. And he never wore anything that was over a year or two old.

He saw her through the glass of the door, and his lips formed her name. She could see in his eyes how much he had missed her, how deeply he regretted letting her go. She knew he really did want her back, wanted to marry her, wanted to give her the commitment she'd always been missing from him. At last.

And it was at that moment, as she met Mark's dark eyes for the first time in weeks, that all the pieces of her own internal puzzle fell into place. She saw Mark— and she knew. She understood completely. She saw at last the secret of her heart, the one she had been keeping from everyone.

Including herself.

She went to the door and pulled it wide. "Hey."

"Hey. Your sister said you were staying back here."

She stepped out of the doorway and ushered him in.

Chapter Fourteen

Jericho sat in the whip three doors down from Ash and Tessa's house.

He stared at the back end of the probably rented Cadillac as the good-looking, pulled-together guy got out of it. The guy went up the front walk and rang the bell. A moment later, the door opened wide and he went in.

Jericho knew who the guy was. Mark. The idiot had finally wised up and come to reclaim what he'd so unbelievably thrown away six weeks ago.

Time to get the hell out. Jericho knew that. He never should have turned onto this street today in the first place. After all, he was supposed to be doing the right damn thing.

But the right thing wasn't working for him. The right thing had kept him awake the night before. That day in the front office, when they were giving her the goodbye cake, the right thing was the last thing on his mind. He'd only wanted to grab her and never let go.

The right thing, impossibly, was starting to seem more and more like the wrong thing. He kept remembering that she'd said she really wanted to stay. That she'd seemed to mean it.

That when she left town, she would be taking his heart with her.

Where, when it all shook out, was the sense in that?

He kept thinking about what Gus had said to him the other day in the coffee shop. That he was being stupid again. He kept thinking, what if Gus was right?

It started to get clear to him that what he'd done by calling it off with her was way too much like a repeat performance of what he'd done a decade ago. He'd told the family not to visit him inside. He'd refused to see Gus or to read Karen's letters. They had lost Karen and he hadn't been there for that. He *should* have been there for that, in spirit if not in the flesh. Karen had deserved that. And so had Gus.

And the family…

He had tried his damnedest to lose his own family. He'd rejected them to punish himself. He'd sent them away and told them not to come around.

Yeah, years later, he got them back again. But what about those years he refused them? That had been so damn stupid. To throw away all those years he could have been with them.

Just like he was throwing Marnie away. Tossing her back to the guy who had dumped her.

How could he be so damn stupid? All over again.

He got out of the whip. He walked fast along the sidewalk and up the driveway, with no real clarity on what he was going to do. Just that he wasn't going to let her go with her ex, not until she knew that he didn't want her to go.

That he loved her. That she was the woman he hadn't even known he'd been waiting for for most of his life.

He was almost to the guesthouse when the door opened. The handsome ex came out, Marnie with him.

Marnie hugged the guy. And then he turned and started toward Jericho. He paused on the walk when they faced each other.

The ex had that look, the one that said he'd lost everything he had tried so damn hard to get back. The ex gave him a nod. Jericho nodded in response.

And that was it. The guy walked on by.

Jericho didn't turn to watch him leave. Marnie had seen him. And he had eyes only for her.

She held out her arms when reached her.

He needed no more encouragement. He grabbed her and held on tight. "You didn't go with him…"

"No. Never. I told you I wouldn't. And *he* understands now. I guess he just needed to hear me say it to his face."

"I should have believed you."

"Yes, you should have. I want to be mad at you for being such a fool. But somehow, I just can't. I… Oh, Jericho. You came back…"

His throat felt like it had a lump the size of Texas in it. He gulped it down. "I never should have left. I thought…it was right, to let you go."

"It was wrong. So wrong…"

"I know. I see that. I know."

She slid her hands up between them, rested her palms against his heart. In her blue eyes, he saw everything. All he'd ever wanted. The two of them. The future. The love he had almost let get away. "I love you," she said. "I knew it when I saw Mark again, that *you* were the one for me. The man I could make a life with. The right man for me."

"You have no idea how good it is to hear that. Marnie, I've been so stupid."

"Oh, yeah." She was nodding. "You have."

He took her hand. "I have more to say. But first, I need to show you something. I need to be certain that you understand."

She looked vaguely alarmed but didn't argue. Or ask any questions. She only nodded.

He turned and started back down the walk, holding firmly to her hand. She followed without hesitation.

He drove her to a neighborhood not far from SA Choppers, a neighborhood that was a little rundown, some of the yards overgrown. He parked in front of his own house, which was gray with white trim.

"Nothing fancy," he said.

She looked at him like he'd just handed her the world. "Your house. It's your house."

"Come on."

They got out and went through the chain-link gate and up the cracked sidewalk. He unlocked the front door and guided her inside ahead of him.

She walked through the empty rooms, her footsteps light and quick on the scuffed hardwood floors. He stayed close behind her.

When she stopped and turned to him, he confessed, "I've got a bedroll. A plastic bowl and a spoon, for cereal in the morning. A coffeemaker, an old stove and a fridge. But you can see there's no furniture. And it's a long way from Olmos Park. Not to mention, Santa Barbara."

A tear spilled over her lower lid and dribbled down her cheek. He gently smudged it away with his thumb.

"If I was in it for the furniture," she said, "I would have stayed with Mark."

He framed her beautiful face in his two rough hands. "Are you sure? You need to be really, really sure."

"I have never been so sure about anything. I want this, I want it with you. I love you. With all my heart. I want to spend my life riding at your side."

And finally, he dared to say the words. "There's no one else for me. You're the one, Marnie Jones. I love you."

With a glad cry, she lifted her arms to him. He gathered her in and he kissed her, a kiss that whispered of forever. A kiss to join two wild, hopeful hearts.

They were married one week later, in an open field, up at the cabin. Gus was best man and Tessa was matron of honor. All the Bravos were there and a large number of Joneses as well. Patrick Jones gave his daughter away with a proud smile and a tear in his eye.

Marnie's Grandpa Oggie raised the first toast at the outdoor party after the ceremony. "To our Marnie, who drove all the way to Texas to find what she was lookin' for. And to Jericho, who had the good sense to be here waitin' when she arrived."

Everyone started clapping. Marnie's wild younger brothers even lit off a couple of illegal firecrackers, which caused Patrick to swear he would tan their hides.

Oggie raised his glass again. "Here's to Jericho and his bride. And above all, here's to love, which is the closest thing to heaven we get here on Earth."

Everyone was quiet then. And a robin's song rose, sweet and high, from a nearby oak branch. Jericho pulled Marnie close.

"I love you," she whispered.

"And I love you. So much. Forever."

It was right, between them. It was good. She was exactly what he'd always wanted, always needed. The road ahead was theirs now. Forever belonged to the two of them, together. He'd found his way home, at last.

* * * * *

Watch for Zoe Bravo's story,
EXPECTING THE BOSS'S BABY,
coming in December 2010,
only from Silhouette Special Edition.
And for you Montana Mavericks fans,
watch for Christine's launch of a
whole new six-book series,
THUNDER CANYON COWBOYS
Coming in July 2010,
wherever Silhouette Special Edition is sold.

Harlequin offers a romance for every mood!
See below for a sneak peek from our paranormal
romance line, Silhouette® Nocturne™.
Enjoy a preview of REUNION by USA TODAY
bestselling author Lindsay McKenna.

Aella closed her eyes and sensed a distinct shift, like movement from the world around her to the unseen world.

She opened her eyes. And had a slight shock at the man standing ten feet away. He wasn't just any man. Her heart leaped and pounded. He reminded her of a fierce warrior from an ancient civilization. Incan? She wasn't sure but she felt his deep power and masculinity.

I'm Aella. Are you the guardian of this sacred site? she asked, hoping her telepathy was strong.

Fox's entire body soared with joy. Fox struggled to put his personal pleasure aside.

Greetings, Aella. I'm the assistant guardian to this sacred area. You may call me Fox. How can I be of service to you, Aella? he asked.

I'm searching for a green sphere. A legend says that the Emperor Pachacuti had seven emerald spheres created for the Emerald Key necklace. He had seven of his priestesses and priests travel the world to hide these spheres from evil forces. It is said that when all seven spheres are found, restrung and worn, that Light will return to the Earth. The fourth sphere is here, at your sacred site. Are you aware of it? Aella held her breath.

She loved looking at him, especially his sensual mouth. The desire to kiss him came out of nowhere.

Fox was stunned by the request. *I know of the Emerald Key necklace because I served the emperor at the time it was created. However, I did not realize that one of the spheres is here.*

Aella felt sad. Why? Every time she looked at Fox, her heart felt as if it would tear out of her chest. *May I stay in touch with you as I work with this site?* she asked.

Of course. Fox wanted nothing more than to be here with her. To absorb her ephemeral beauty and hear her speak once more.

Aella's spirit lifted. What *was* this strange connection between them? Her curiosity was strong, but she had more pressing matters. In the next few days, Aella knew her life would change forever. How, she had no idea….

Look for REUNION
by USA TODAY *bestselling author*
Lindsay McKenna,
available April 2010,
only from Silhouette® Nocturne™.

Silhouette®

SPECIAL EDITION

INTRODUCING A BRAND-NEW MINISERIES FROM *USA TODAY* BESTSELLING AUTHOR

KASEY MICHAELS

SECOND-CHANCE BRIDAL

At twenty-eight, widowed single mother Elizabeth Carstairs thinks she's left love behind forever....until she meets Will Hollingsbrook. Her sons' new baseball coach is the handsomest man she's ever seen—and the more time they spend together, the more undeniable the connection between them. But can Elizabeth leave the past behind and open her heart to a second chance at love?

FIND OUT IN

SUDDENLY A BRIDE

*Available in April
wherever books are sold.*

Love Inspired

Single father Ian Ferguson's
daughter is finally coming
out of her shell thanks to the
twenty-three-year-old tutor
Alexa Michaels. Although
Alexa is young—and too
pretty—she graduated from
the school of hard knocks
and is challenging some of
Ian's old-school ways. Could
this dad learn some valuable
lessons about love, family
and faith from the least
likely teacher?

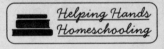

Look for

Love Lessons

by

Margaret Daley

*Available April
wherever books are sold.*

Steeple
Hill®

www.SteepleHill.com

LI87590

ROMANCE, RIVALRY
AND A FAMILY REUNITED

THE BRIDES
of
BELLA ROSA

William Valentine and his beloved wife, Lucia, live
a beautiful life together, but when his former love Rosa
and the secret family they had together resurface,
an instant rivalry is formed. Can these families
get through the past and come together as one?

Step into the world of Bella Rosa
beginning this April with

Beauty and the Reclusive Prince
by

RAYE MORGAN

Eight volumes to collect and treasure!

HARLEQUIN®

INTRIGUE®

WILL THIS REUNITED FAMILY
BE STRONG ENOUGH TO EXPOSE
A LURKING KILLER?

FIND OUT IN THIS ALL-NEW
THRILLING TRILOGY FROM TOP
HARLEQUIN INTRIGUE AUTHOR

B.J. DANIELS

WHITEHORSE
MONTANA

Winchester Ranch

GUN-SHY BRIDE—*April 2010*

HITCHED—*May 2010*

TWELVE-GAUGE GUARDIAN—
June 2010

2 Stories in 1

HER MEDITERRANEAN PLAYBOY

Sexy and dangerous—he wants you in his bed!

The sky is blue, the azure sea is crashing
against the golden sand and the sun is hot.

The conditions are perfect for
a scorching Mediterranean seduction
from two irresistible untamed playboys!

Indulge your senses with these two delicious stories

A MISTRESS AT THE ITALIAN'S COMMAND
by *Melanie Milburne*

ITALIAN BOSS, HOUSEKEEPER MISTRESS
by *Kate Hewitt*

Available April 2010 from Harlequin Presents!

www.eHarlequin.com

HP12910

HARLEQUIN
Ambassadors

Want to share your passion for reading Harlequin® Books?

Become a Harlequin Ambassador!

Harlequin Ambassadors are a group
of passionate and well-connected readers
who are willing to share their joy of reading
Harlequin® books with family and friends.

You'll be sent all the tools you need to spark
great conversation, including free books!

All we ask is that you share the romance
with your friends and family!

You'll also be invited to have a say in
new book ideas and exchange opinions
with women just like you!

**To see if you qualify* to be
a Harlequin Ambassador, please visit
www.HarlequinAmbassadors.com.**

*Please note that not everyone who applies to be a Harlequin Ambassador will
qualify. For more information please visit www.HarlequinAmbassadors.com.

Thank you for your participation.

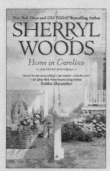
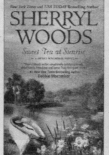

REQUEST YOUR FREE BOOKS!
2 FREE NOVELS PLUS 2 FREE GIFTS!

SPECIAL EDITION
Life, Love and Family!

SSE10